ELIZABETH HARDWICK

was born in Lexington, Kentucky in 1916, and graduated from
the University of Kentucky in 1939. She did post-graduate work
at Columbia from 1939 to 1941 and was Adjunct Professor of
Barnard College. She was awarded a Guggenheim Fellowship in
1947, the George Nathan Award for Dramatic Criticism in 1966,
is a member of the American Academy and Institute of Art and
Letters and has contributed regularly to *Partisan Review*,
Harpers and the *New Yorker*. Her works include three novels,
The Ghostly Lover (1945), *The Simple Truth* (1955) and
Sleepless Nights (1979), and two collections of essays, *A View of
My Own* (1962) and *Seduction and Betrayal* (1974). She is also
the editor of *The Selected Letters of William James* (1960).
Elizabeth Hardwick was married to the poet Robert Lowell from
1949–1972. A founder and Advisory Editor of the *New York
Review of Books*, she lives in New York.

Virago publishes *Sleepless Nights* and *The Ghostly Lover*, and
will publish *The Simple Truth* in 1987.

VIRAGO
MODERN
CLASSIC

NUMBER
41

SLEEPLESS NIGHTS

Elizabeth Hardwick

Virago

Published by VIRAGO Limited 1980
41 William IV Street, London WC2N 4DB

Reprinted 1986

First published in Great Britain by
Weidenfeld and Nicolson Ltd. 1979

British Library Cataloguing in Publication Data
Hardwick, Elizabeth
Sleepless nights. –
(Virago modern classic).
I. Title
823'.9'1F   PS3515.A5672S
ISBN 0-86068-189-0

Printed in Great Britain by
Anchor Brendon Ltd. of Tiptree, Essex

To my daughter, Harriet,
  and
to my friend, Mary McCarthy

SLEEPLESS NIGHTS

Part One

IT IS JUNE. This is what I have decided to do with my life just now. I will do this work of transformed and even distorted memory and lead this life, the one I am leading today. Every morning the blue clock and the crocheted bedspread with its pink and blue and gray squares and diamonds. How nice it is —this production of a broken old woman in a squalid nursing home. The niceness and the squalor and sorrow in an apathetic battle—that is what I see. More beautiful is the table with the telephone, the books and magazines, the *Times* at the door, the birdsong of rough, grinding trucks in the street.

If only one knew what to remember or pretend to remember. Make a decision and what you want from the lost things will present itself. You can take it down like a can from a shelf. Perhaps. One can would be marked Rand Avenue in Kentucky and some would recall the address at least as true. Inside the can are the blackening porches of winter, the gas grates, the swarm.

The sunlight blinds me. When I look up I see confusing electricity behind windows. Maybe the shadows will suffice, the light and the shade. Think of yourself as if you were in Apollinaire's poem:

Here you are in Marseilles, surrounded by watermelons.
Here you are in Coblenz at the Hotel du Géant.
Here you are in Rome sitting under a Japanese medlar tree.
Here you are in Amsterdam . . .

1954
Dearest M.: Here I am in Boston, on Marlborough Street, number 239. I am looking out on a snowstorm. It fell like a great armistice, bringing all simple struggles to an end. In the extraordinary snow, people are walking about in wonderful costumes—old coats with fur collars, woolen caps, scarves, boots, leather hiking shoes that shine like copper. Under the yellow glow of the streetlights you begin to imagine what it was like forty or fifty years ago. The stillness, the open whiteness—nostalgia and romance in the clear, quiet, white air . . .

More or less settled in this handsome house. Flowered curtains made to measure, rugs cut for the stairs, bookshelves, wood for the fireplace. Climbing up and down the four floors gives you a sense of ownership—perhaps. It may be yours, but the house, the furniture, strain toward the universal and it will soon read like a stage direction: Setting—Boston. The law will be obeyed. Chests, tables, dishes, domestic habits fall into line.

Beautiful mantles of decorated marble—neo-Greek

designs of fading blacks and palest greens. "Worth the price of the whole house"—the seller's flourish of opinion, and true for once. But it is the whole house that occupies my thoughts. On the second floor, two parlors. Grand, yes, but 239 is certainly not without its pockets of deprivation, its corners of tackiness. Still, it is a setting.

Here I am with my hibiscus blooming in the bay window. The other parlor looks out on the alley between Marlborough and Beacon. There an idiot man keeps a dog on a chain, day and night. Bachelor garbage, decay, bewilderment pile up around the man. I have the idea he once had a family, but they have gone away. I imagine that if the children were to visit he would say, "Come to see the dog on a chain. It is a present." In the interest of the dog I call the police. The man glances up at my window in perturbation, wondering what he has done wrong. Darwin wrote someplace that the suffering of the lower animals throughout time was more than he could bear to think of.

> Dearest love,
> Elizabeth

The beginning of June was hot. I took a journey, and of course, immediately everything was new. When you travel your first discovery is that you do not exist. The phlox bloomed in its faded purples; on the hillside, phallic pines. Foreigners under the arcades, in the basket shops. A steamy haze blurred the lines of the hills. A dirty, exhausting sky. Already the summer seemed to be passing away. Soon the boats would be gathered in, ferries roped to the dock.

Looking for the fosselized, for something—persons and places thick and encrusted with final shape; instead there are many, many minnows, wildly swimming, trembling, vigilant to escape the net.

Kentucky: that is certainly part of it. My mother lived as a girl in so many North Carolina towns they are confused in my memory. Raleigh and Charlotte. She hardly knew her own parents; they died quickly as people did then, of whatever was in the air—pneumonia, diptheria, tuberculosis. I never knew a person so indifferent to the past. It was as if she did not know who she was. She had brothers and sisters and was raised by them, passing their names down to us.

Her face, my mother's, is not clear to me. A boneless, soft prettiness, with small brown eyes and the scarcest of eyebrows, darkened with a lead pencil.

1962
Dearest M.: Here I am back in New York, on 67th Street in a high, steep place with long, dirty windows. In the late afternoon, in the gloom of the winter sky, I sometimes imagine it is Edinburgh in the nineties. I have never been to Edinburgh, but I like cities of reasonable size, provincial capitals. Still it is definitely New York here, underfoot and overhead. The passage from Boston was not easy. Not unlike a crossing of the ocean, or of the country itself—all your things to be dragged over the mountains. I can say that the trestle table and the highboy were ill-prepared for the sudden exile, the change of government as it was in a way for me. Well, fumed oak stands in the corner, bottles and ice bucket on top. Five of the Naval Academy plates are broken. The clocks have had their terminal stroke and will never again know life. The old bureaus stand fixed, humiliated, chipped.

Displaced things and old people, rigid, with their tired veins and clogged arteries, with their bunions and aching arches, their sparse hair and wavering thoughts, over the Carpathian Mountains, out of the bayous—that is what it is like here in the holy city. Aunt Lotte's portrait will never be unpacked again. She finds her resting place in the tomb of her crate, in the basement, her requiem the humming of the Seventh Avenue subway.

Of course these things are not *mine*. I think they are usually spoken of as *ours*, that tea bag of a word which steeps in the conditional.

    Love, love,
      Elizabeth

"Beginnings are always delightful; the threshold is the place to pause," Goethe said. New York once more, to remain forever, resting on its generous accommodation of women. Long dresses, arrogance, more chances to deceive the deceitful, confidants, conspirators, charge cards.

I was then a "we." He is teasing, smiling, drinking gin after a long day's work, saying something like this to the air:

The tyranny of the weak is a burdensome thing and yet it is better to be exploited by the weak than by the strong . . . Submission to the powerful is a redundancy and very fatiguing and boring in the end. There is nothing subtle or interesting in it . . . mainly because the exercise is too frequent. A workout in the morning, another in the evening . . . Husband-wife: not a new move to be discovered in that strong classical tradition. Arguments are like the grinding of rusty blades, the old motor and its troublesome knockings. The dog growls. He too knows his lines.

Can it be that I am the subject?

True, with the weak something is always happening: improvisation, surprise, suspense, injustice, manipulation, hypochondria, secret drinking, jealousy, lying, crying, hiding in the garden, driving off in the middle of the night. The weak have the purest sense of history. Anything can happen. Each one of them is a palmist, reading his own hand. Yes, I will either have a long or a short life; he (she) will be either blond or dark-haired.

Tickets, migrations, worries, property, debts, changes of name and changes back once more: these came about from reading many books. So, from Kentucky to New York, to Boston, to Maine, to Europe, carried along on a river of paragraphs and chapters, of blank verse, of little books translated from the Polish, large books from the Russian—all consumed in a sedentary sleeplessness. Is that sufficient—never mind that it is the truth. It certainly hasn't the drama of: I saw the old, white-bearded frigate master on the dock and signed up for the journey. But after all, "I" am a woman.

I find myself on the train from Montreal to Kingston. I am going to the university for a few days—and not so long ago. It is a Sunday night, deep winter, and we push on through the cold, black emptiness. Sometimes the bronze glow of a distant car light shines in the distance, flickers like a candle on the curves. The train seems to be always going straight ahead in the lucky, large, empty country.

It is only a few degrees above zero, but in the club car we are in the midst of a sensual, tropical heat, a masculine heat of some kind. I am the only woman in car number 50.

They are very noisy. A perfunctory noise and a good deal of the spurious laughter of a group together too long. The men are in a forced holiday condition, nearing the falling, dying end of it. Most are drunk and more than one looks sick. Canadians, do not vomit on me! It appears they have been to a meeting, a convention. They are bound together by occupation; perhaps they sell something. they are certainly not greatly prosperous; no, certainly not. I am sure of that from my unworthy calculations based on the arithmetic of snobbery and shame.

"Shame is inventive," Nietzsche said. And that is scarcely the half of it. From shame I have paid attention to clothes, shoes, rings, watches, accents, teeth, points of deportment, turns of speech. The men on the train are wearing clothes which, made for no season, are therefore always unseasonable and contradictory. They are harsh and flimsy, loud and yet lightweight, fashioned with the inappropriateness that is the ruling idea of the year-round. Pastels blue as the sea and green as the land; jackets lined with paisley and plaid; seams outlined with wide stitches of another color; revers and pockets outsize; predominance of chilly blue and two-tones; nylon and Dacron in the as-smooth-as-glass finish of the permanently pressed. On the other hand, the porters from Trinidad are traditional, dressed like princes. Black trousers, red cotton jacket, white shirt, black bow tie and black, luminous, aristocratic, tropical faces.

The men are very white, very fair, and even their nut-brown hair lies over a reddish-blond brow. Their whiteness reminds me that they are truly my brothers, going home to my sisters, my sisters-in-law. The presence of the men makes me uneasy; one of them stirs my memory because of the small chip in a front tooth that brings back a woeful night on the sofa in a fraternity house. Another has taken off a tight shoe and sits for a long time voluptuously staring at his liberated foot. Not one is a stranger, so near are the pale eyes, the part in the hair, the touching, sluggish hilarity.

Borges asks the question: "Are not the fervent Shakespeareans who give themselves over to a line of Shakespeare, are they not, literally, Shakespeare?"

Here, rushing on through the black night, these men with their bright clothes, under the waning moon of their drunkenness, mingle with my own flesh, as if I had been in the back seat of a car with each of them, had "pored over" their unsettled text. Men with red-lined eyes, heavy high school signet rings, white cotton undershirts, days at the filling station preparing to face the labor for those families that are from their first youth already in their eyes.

The club car, now rattling with debris, raced backward. A gate whined on its rusty hook, an old car and truck stood in the gravel, the door closes on my own brothers and sisters slipping in late to fall silently on one of the many beds with pleasant depressions in the middle. The sighs and tears, the shouts of injustice, all the destinies linked by a likeness of forehead and nose, by irresistible sympathies and such distances that each one gorged on a petty vanity, the fantasy of being an orphan.

*   *   *

Pasternak's line: *To live a life is not to cross a field*. It is not to climb a mountain either. Leconte de Lisle spoke enviously of Victor Hugo as having the "stupidity of the Himalayas." The murderous German girl with her alpenstock, her hiking boots, calls to the old architect, higher, higher! He falls to his death and this is Ibsen's disgust with the giddiness up there, or the assumption of up there. For himself, he adjusted his rimless spectacles and the corners of his mouth turned down when fervent young girls thought he was dumber than he was. Ibsen was not a happy man. Work all day, more than a little schnapps in the evening, and back home at the hotel, the resort, the pension there was his strong wife who after she had little Sigurd Ibsen said: That's it, that's enough.

Neither more nor less straight across the field, destination the clump of trees or the stone fence that ends your property; nor upward slowly, often out of breath. Yet, profound changes and removals along the line split the spirit apart. Where is Vermont or Minnesota after you have packed up your things and taken your old wife to Florida—to live, to live, without the furnace and the snowplow? While you are living, part of you has slipped away to the cemetery.

Kentucky, Lexington; the university, Henry Clay High School, Main Street. The cemetery of home, education, nerves, heritage and tics. Fading, it is sad; remaining, it is a needle. Trees, flowers, noble old houses, triumphant farms on the outskirts of town—little distraction to the heart in that before the antiquarian interests of middle age. Store clerks and waitresses are the heroines of my memories, those ladies cast off with children to raise; they keep things open, light up the night on Main Street, that paradisiacal center of towns then. Woolworth's, the cigar store, three segregated movie houses, two sensual hotels where the wastebaskets contained memorandums of assignations and the hyperbolic, misshapen prose of illicit love letters.

It is not true that it doesn't matter where you live, that you are in Hartford or Dallas merely yourself. Also it is not true that all are linked naturally to their regions. Many are flung down carelessly at birth and they experience the diminishment and sometimes the pleasant truculence of their random misplacement. Americans who are Germans, Germans who are Frenchmen, like Heine perhaps.

The stain of place hangs on not as a birthright but as a sort of artifice, a bit of cosmetic. I place myself among the imports, those jarring and jarred pieces that sit in the closet among the matching china sets. I have no relations that I know of born outside the South and hardly any living outside it even today. Nevertheless, I am afraid of the country night and its honest slumbers, uneasy even in the daylight with "original settlers" and old American stock. The highway, the asphalt paths, the thieves, the contaminated skies like a suffocating cloak of mangy fur, the millions in their boroughs—that is truly home.

I have always, all of my life, been looking for help from a man. It has come many times and many more it has not. This began early. We, several girls from the neighborhood, met a very nice-looking old man, not dressed like our own people, but a gentleman in a black suit and white shirt, wearing a kind and courtly smile. He was indeed kind and courtly. He waited for us on Saturday afternoons, paid our way into the movie, bought us the whitened, hardened chocolate of summer. In the dark, with a little girl on each side, sitting as straight as caryatids, he ran his hand up our thighs, under our dresses. The predator's first gift, mixed with the bright narrative on the screen and with the chocolate, was to reveal early to us the tangled nature of bribery. This at least was a lasting lesson. Bribery and more bribery—it grows within you like your molars. Another truly broken old man, poor, ignorant, with a rotten, rooty old grocery store like a cellar, handed out scum-covered pickles and soggy gingersnaps.

Lexington, the Bluegrass. Man o' War on view. His large melancholy skull only dimly remembered his celebrated stands as stud. As a sight, this great horse had some of the blank statistical superiority of the Pyramids. Horses. Their images everywhere, on calendars, on ashtrays. The paddock narratives on the walls of saloons. Wrinkled, broken jockeys with faces like the shell of a nut. Luckless bettors, flamboyant afternoons of the spring and fall meets.

1940
Dear Mama: I love Columbia. Of course I do. The best people here are all Jews—what you call "Hebrews." There is a not very interesting young man from Harvard who wears a lot of gray, a heavy, pedantic Middle Westerner, a disappointing star from Vassar. They are all very much admired by the faculty because they aren't too smart . . .

Mother and father are soon dead. That is what it all comes to, but do they see their own death as the loss of mother and father? I remember our resistant garden, planted with the recalcitrant, stupidly demanding gladiolus which, after terrible spoiling, yield their pinkish-orange goblets; and the retarded dahlia, forever procrastinating, finally blooming in its liverish purples.

Seasons of nature and seasons of experience that appear as a surprise but are merely the arrival of the calendar's predictions. Thus the full moon of excited churchgoing days and the frost of apostasy as fourteen arrives. One climbs on the weather vane and looks at the heavens and then, pausing for a moment, falls off.

The Presbyterian church was agreeable in winter, with its damp cloakrooms and its snowy-haired superintendents, its subdued hymnal and discreet baptism. More memorable and disturbing were surreptitious visits to itinerant evangelical tent meetings. There it was possible to be saved more than once, saved again and again. Yes, I accept Jesus Christ as my personal Savior on the west side of town in June, accept Christ once more in the scorched field in the North End in July, and then again on the campgrounds to the south in August. Lots of the saved ones, weaving up to the front, gathered under the rhythmical arms and gold cuff links of the preacher, have just come out of the penitentiary.

Under the string of light bulbs in the humid tents, the desperate and unsteady human wills struggle for a night against the fierce pessimism of experience and the root empiricism of every troubled loser. The hour of tranquillity seems so near to the balm of the vices that propel the needy through the open canvas flaps of conversion. Careworn spirits with faces hard to love: dry, curled, brown-gray hair caught up in nets, eyeglasses serviceable and pasted early on young faces; posture slumped, rounded, the flesh and bone thrown out of line by diffidence, failure, and the blank glare of square bungalows without shade.

Perhaps here began a prying sympathy for the victims of sloth and recurrent mistakes, sympathy for the tendency of lives to obey the laws of gravity and to sink downward, falling as gently and slowly as a kite, or violently breaking, smashing.

The apotheosis of a local teaching certificate, a celestial and long-delayed reward for girls. To become a sacerdotal offering, very much like those pale schoolteachers in Latin America, men from the poor villages, sweating in their black suits and white shirts, receiving and giving a peculiar list of punishments in their visionary calling.

There was a man who brought me my first pair of reading glasses, which I did not need. He was a romantic figure, mostly because he had studied French and adored the difficult *r*'s of that language. He was tall and good-looking and not very truthful. He was corrupted by an uncertain nature and no one understood his fits of self-expansion or his disappearances into torpor and melancholy. And yet a vanity and rather pleasant carelessness seemed to survive in all his moods.

This man spoke of his attraction to "experience" and I gathered that what is meant is an attraction to something contrary to oneself, usually a being or habit lower, more dangerous, risky. His experience included a forgotten marriage, entanglements with waitresses, hairdressers, women who sold tobacco at the hotel, drifting, pretty women, all losers. One of his passions was for educating women, and he spoke to them of his interests at that time —James Branch Cabell and the poems of Verlaine. He bore a great name whose dignity extended throughout our county. The members of his family were alarmed by his pretensions. Strolling about Main Street, blond and tall and coarse as a Goth, he presented himself as a sensual aesthete, Southern, intellectual in the University of Virginia manner. His hunger for experience was not so much deep as wide. Like an actor he created spaces around himself, and when others were talking there was an arranged, dramatic silence drawn across his face.

When I think back, he is wearing brown. Coming toward me. We are near the library, in the shade of old trees, near a peaceful house with a walled garden. Gothic revival, white columns in the distance. Everything washed in a harsh, hard light. He is thirty and I am eighteen. No power of mind can decipher why the difference in our ages defined everything to me, cast over every clarity a dark and sinister puzzle. There in the light, his exorbitant desire to please. Large, square teeth and something of the useless energy of a large, affectionate dog. The leap and lunge of his greeting.

His curiosity flamed over a word, an adjective over the seductiveness of the fact that I was taking down a volume of Thomas Mann from the library shelves. Eros has a thousand friends.

His car was beautiful, black, with a canvas top and sides. From our first meeting he would drive me home and drop me at the corner of our street, a block or so from my house. The action signaled his love of the illicit, his need to infect the scene with the fumes of a mésalliance. Throw out a corrupting ambiguity, also.

He took me on a Saturday afternoon soon after to a

sodden, threatening part of town, under the railroad tracks, a sullen little settlement beside a viaduct. A treeless, almost outlawed part of town I scarcely knew the name of. Old cats, lazing in the sun, misbegotten dogs; in the midst of it a new, square white church, like a garage. Outside suspicious-looking women were laying out picnic tables for a gathering the next day. He smiled at the women with hungry interest. Smiling, bowing, the car shining in the sun, his face alive with glee as if he had come upon precious material, material of life. Daring, greedy smile.

The church women, hunched with the weight of their aberrant, consuming sectarianism, looked back at him, eyes dead, Pentecostal fires banked. Didactic downturn of the religious mouth. And yet the brown suit, the large, lapping dog face, impressed for a moment. Suspicion returned as we went into a house across the road.

It had two rooms. I stepped into them with the feeling of falling into a well of disgrace. That tender, warning word *disgrace* I carried about with me for years and years; it has its reasonable, scolding power over me still. It freezes the radical heart with lashing whispers. Someone lived in the little house. A woman. Scents and powders and in the corner a pair of quilted slippers.

I did not struggle. I did not ask questions. Moral unease hurt, but the pain was the pain of eternity and not to be made too much of. He came down on top of me, smiling, courteous, determined. When he let me out at the corner I raced home to a house filled with people near to desperation.

For him, some years later he went with a girl to a lake in eastern Kentucky and there suddenly jumped off a high bridge. I inquired. No, he was not depressed. Rather, the opposite. He jumped to his death on the high, as it were, filled with a brave elation, a genuine, rare carelessness.

Sometimes the rain was beautiful. The lavender and silver streaks, gleaming in the mud, seek to be honored, to receive some word of gratitude. The kindness of damp afternoons, the solace of opening the door and finding everyone there.

What next? Where to? Even in the midst of it all, in the devoted warmth, the well-disposed threat of familiarity, the cemetery waits to be desecrated.

Farewell to Kentucky and our agreeable vices. We go to bed early, but because of whiskey seldom with a clear head. We are fond of string beans and thin slices of salty ham. When I left home my brother said: It will be wonderful if you make a success of life, then you can follow the races.

Farewell to the precious limestone, to the dynasties of swift horse bones. But it was a long, drawn-out parting. I was bewitched by my mother and would wake up on 116th Street in New York longing for the sight of her round, soft curves, her hair twisted into limp curls at the temples, her weight on the stepladder washing windows, her roasts and potatoes and fat yeast rolls; and her patient breathing in the back room as she lay sleeping in a lumpy old feather bed.

In graduate school at Columbia I met a girl who had grown up on a rich person's estate on Long Island, a place owned by lazy, fashionable people. My friend's father was a gardener and her mother was a cook. It seemed to me that this condition was rich with interest, that the girl inhabited a lighthouse from which could be seen a great deal that was meant to be hidden, hidden at least from clever, critical, and bookish girls. She was certainly not inclined to a hopeless emulation nor easily moved to admiration. Her eyes, suspicious as the cool glance of a detective, would be quick to find hypocrisy, bizarre inclinations. No, this girl's whole life was scarred by her residential fate; her brilliance was unaccommodating and she was bitter, wild with rage and, alas, a dour envy.

In her twisted little heart the blood beat with hatred when the cars drove up the drive. She, with her passionate reading of Proust and James, nevertheless hated the very smell of the rich evening air, loathed the unsettling drawl of debutantes. But her deepest resentment beat down upon her family, upon the humbling thought of her father's gardening shears at the hedge. Tragedy for her in the swish, swish of her mother in her rubber-soled nurses' shoes, bending forward with a bowl of vegetables resting expertly on her open palm. In truth here was a great spirit destroyed by Long Island feudalism; a knotty, angry peasant reared in a Southampton cottage.

I tried to make her a radical, but there was no mercy in her. Instead, grinding away in rage for her Ph.D., she became or decided that she was a lesbian. In a frightened, angry plunge, she fell into a desperate affair with a handsome older woman from England. And what did she find there? Happiness, consolation? No, she found, with her ineluctable ill-luck, a nightmare of betrayals, lies, deceits, shocks, infidelities, dismissals. All the rusty arrows hit their mark. And she gave forth again her sad and piercing cry—*ah, perfido!*

Part Two

EVERYTHING groans under treachery. The yellow, thirsting grass when the rain betrays it day after day without mercy, and the sun all the while smiling away in the sky for brown legs and warm water for ungrateful swimmers. At times, thinking of the unfortunate ones I have known, it seems to me that they live surrounded by their kind. The windows resent their curtains, the light its woven shade, the door its lock, the coffin its loathsome, suffocating pile of dirt. But what can they do? The grass shrugs, the windows grow sullen, the light gives out a sardonic glow, the door swells and requires a shoulder to push it open, the coffin hibernates in a long, not displeasing slumber.

Anyway at that time I loved to go back and forth between New York and home—to see what I knew was there. A cold snap in the winter, redbud in the spring, teeth of so many pulled out just after childhood. The mysterious nuns at the old St. Joseph hospital taking temperatures. My mind is shaken by the memory of early deaths, boys from high school, girls also. *Drinking himself to death*: I could name many who did not reach twenty-five.

Other deaths. A neighborhood girl or young woman, for whom we all felt an intense pity and wonder, a shiver of symbolism, as if she were one who in a peculiar, blighted way suffered for many. She represented the fallen state too vividly and fortuitously to be endured. This girl became a prostitute and without any clear economic necessity. But reason not the need.

She spent her nights in the most sordid and degrading dumps and rooming houses. She wandered around raw saloons near the old railroad station. She was the much-loved daughter of a railroad worker who wore his blue-and-white denim cap and took the union newspaper. Her mother was large, tall, hardworking; her grandmother was fair, tall and smoked a corncob pipe. Juanita! Juanita! they sang out to her, their only child, calling her to lunch, to rest. When she was still in high school, before her "career" began, she stood around in the yard a lot, pulling on the thick, kinky curls that nestled near the collar of her freshly ironed dress.

She grew tall and rather nondescript. She developed a refusal to meet your glance and therefore a striking, not unattractive, awkwardness overcame her when she met someone from the neighborhood. She drank, she aged, she suffered terribly from her dissipations. Throughout all her tears and pains she was carefully, patiently nursed by her family.

After midnight we could hear a car door slam on the street behind us. Sometimes Juanita was brought home by the decrepit taxis that stood all night in their place downtown. The yellow lights would shine out in the darkness as the car slowly crept homeward. Or walking alone, down the narrow, dark, moon-shadowed lane she moved swiftly, her heels clicking on the pavement, her cough quick and shallow. At last the screen door of Juanita's house slammed gently. No doubt the old people turned in their beds with relief. Home at last was the tall, curly-haired, curious voluptuary; asleep once more the swollen and coarsened daughter. It all had to be paid for by Juanita, every penny of the cost. She wept from hang-overs, from misery, from confusion, the terrible confusion of a distorted world that was darkening around her. And finally she wept from venereal disease. Sympathy and be-wilderment among all the women in her house. Juanita is not feeling well today, her raw-boned mother, large and neat in a long, full housedress, would say. Maybe she's catching a little cold. Scornfully the neighbors would say: She's caught more than a little cold this time.

Not too many years later Juanita died of prodigious pains and sores; she went out in unbelievable suffering.

I like to remember the patience of old spinsters, some that looked like sea captains with their clear blue eyes, hair of soft, snowy whiteness, dazzling cheerfulness. Soli-tary music teachers, themselves bred on toil, leading the young by way of pain and discipline to their own honor-able impasse, teaching in that way the scales of disap-pointment.

The paradox of the woman who reaches her true spin-sterhood only after she is at last married and settled. She takes command and reaches a state of dominating de-pendency to which only she has the clue. How confident her reign, how skillful the solitary diplomacy, the ordering of the future and control of the present. She gathers in revenues and makes dispensations, carefully, never forgetting that she is alone.

Or when spinsters come in pairs, sometimes brothers and sisters, Clifford and Hepzibah. Beneath the pruderies and reticence, the humble acquiescence, the thin authority, the veils of a legendary *chagrin d'amour*, lovers unknown killed in wars: a tremendous turbulence rushes forth in season. Northern lights, comets.

Society tries to write these lives before they are lived. It does not always succeed. I have known from home the anarchic sexual secrets of plain, unmarried schoolteachers, some with their thick savings accounts, their accumulation of house lots and rooming houses, their hoarded legacies from parents, aunts and uncles. Often these women tricked fate by their hidden inclination to men of bad character, younger than themselves: a yard man, a drifter, ex-convict. Gentlemen do not appeal to all women.

Je t'adore brigand.

My own affectionate, tireless mother had nine children. This fateful fertility kept her for most of her life under the dominion of nature. It was a thing, a presence, and she seemed to walk about encased in the clear globe of it. It was what she was always doing, and in the end what she had done.

Sometimes in the dark of my own nights her life would come back to me. When the counterpane was thrown aside, the light of the Hotel Empire shining red through the bamboo slats. Love and alcohol and the clothes on the floor; perfumes. No, no it was impossible that it was the same. Impersonal history, that which spreads over all, had altered the bedroom, the lovemaking.

My mother's femaleness was absolute, ancient, and there was a peculiar, helpless assertiveness about it. Not the assertiveness of opinion, for she seemed to have no opinion about it and would, even when she was past seventy, merely shrug and looked perplexed when the subject of her own childbearing was raised. Or sometimes she might say: It did not make me miserable, if that's what you want to know.

The assertiveness was merely the old, profound acceptance of the things of life. It was modest, smooth and soft as a handful of cotton. Without plan, without provision. All of that comes later as the body and even the soul go about the daily caring for the results of this seemingly natural acceptance.

And she was nothing at all like the cheeerful twos and threes of the 1950's, all of them living out their decade in the new station wagon, off to the camping site, the beach, the weekend, with the dog and the cat, the summer house and the camera.

An ineffable femininity, tidal. Mortification in the face of these oceanic rhythms was the unspoken, perhaps unconscious, lot of the children who expressed it in their passionate love for their kind, happy mother and in a singularly low birthrate for themselves.

Flaubert wrote in a letter to Louise Colet that he could never see a cradle without thinking of a grave.

During the joy of New York I was still for many years drawn back home. Christmas visits down to Lexington, carried in the womb of the George Washington Pullman cars on the old C&O. I—wearing a putative mink from the Ritz Thrift Shop on 57th Street. The train passed through mining towns in West Virginia, down through Ashland, Kentucky, through Olive Hill and Morehead. A stinging, empty, country stillness along the way, the hills rising up on either side to cradle the train as it slipped through the valley. Square, leaning cabins, clinging like mountain goats; ribbons of wood smoke drifting in the mist. Trail of the Lonesome Pine, Little Shepherd of Kingdom Come, the disreputable, whining vowels and diphthongs of the mountain people.

Once back home, my thought was: Do not speak to me of horses, of the Kentucky Derby. In school I remember that an unlikely radical in the Agricultural College did a study which seemed to prove that the costly offspring of thoroughbreds, auctioned off each year, did not bring in any more money, win more races, than the genuises from the lower horse classes—those blessed mathematicians whose fathers ran candy stores. The joys of the Enlightenment.

Still I remember the old race track, before Keeneland was built, before the barns burned and the horses screamed all night in their prisons. A pastoral quality then, something theatrical and marginal, like the coming of the circus. The lustrous afternoons, faded blue paled by sunlight, the soft May air. The tracks at dawn, the early sun, the tranquil curve of the empty grandstands.

Near the end of the afternoon the important race is finally run. The purity of the dawn is forgotten. The dogwood and the lilac droop in the chill. And then the stress of the race, the pain and the pleasure of the outrageous effort are finally consecrated in a few moments. The sacrificial power of the horse and its Faustian contract with the jockey—something can be learned from that. A *tristesse* falls down upon the scene, down on the old memory. The horses are led away to their rest, their feelings about the race they have run unknown to us.

Perhaps it is true that being from where I am I was born a gambler. And as the gambler in Dostoevsky's great story says: It is true that only one out of a hundred wins, but what is that to me?

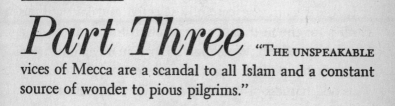

Part Three "THE UNSPEAKABLE
vices of Mecca are a scandal to all Islam and a constant
source of wonder to pious pilgrims."

For the pilgrim to Mecca the life of the city trembled
with its dangerous salvations.

1940's
New York: there I lived at the Hotel Schuyler on West
45th Street, lived with a red-cheeked, homosexual young
man from Kentucky. We had known each other all our
lives. Our friendship was a violent one and we were as
obsessive, critical, jealous and cruel as any ordinary couple.
The rages, the slamming doors, the silences, the dis-
sembling. Each was for the other a treasured object of
gossip and complaint. In spite of his inclinations, the
drama was of man and woman, a genetic dissonance so
like the marital howlings one could hear floating up from

the courtyard or creeping up and down the rusty fire escapes.

The sharing of premises, premises laid out in these hotels with a brilliant economy that could make of strangers a mock family and turn a family into strangers. This sharing was all "living together" meant between us. And yet the grating friendship flowered in the morning and withered at night, shriveled in the winter and blossomed once more in the spring.

Often I lay awake fretting over some delinquency of J.'s. His coercive neatness inflamed me at times, as if his habits were not his right, but instead a dangerous poison to life, like the slow seepage of gas from the hotel stove.

In the evening he carefully selected and laid out his clothes for the next day; a preparation for going off to a much-despised job. Worst of all, J. had an unyielding need to brush his perfect teeth after dinner in the evening. This odd harness of habit held him in a vicious embrace and finally meant that no fortuitous invitation, no beguiling possibility arising unannounced could be accepted without a concentrated uneasiness of mind. These sacred routines did much to inhibit his sex life, even though he was, like the tolling of a bell, to be found every Saturday night at certain gay bars, drinking his rigid ration of beer.

Dear J.: Now you would be in an intense middle age if the carelessness of others had not annihilated in an instant all of your martyrdom to detail. A car went out of control at a crossing in Los Angeles and struck him down, he who was patiently observing the traffic lights. Hard not to imagine that the car, released from the oppression of brakes and the tyranny of a king at the steering wheel, malevolently rushed into an ecstatic terrorism against J.'s neat, clerkly life at the curb.

Even now I can still hear J. singing in a thin, pure tenor with a hint in it of the mountains, where his family came from. He greatly feared his father, a large, large, fair man in black clothes, a country businessman. When the father died, the state government sent a police escort to the funeral and the mountain people stood staring in the streets. J. greatly cared for his mother—classic that he was—although of the two the father was the more interesting, but too large, clothes too black, white shirts too starchy, collar too stiff.

I remember when I first toddled into his office, J. would say, a queer from my first breath, and knew that I had been dealt a wrong card—this man weighing three hundred pounds, sitting behind a roll-top desk. I'm told I screamed like the girl I was.

At home, as a clever and by some richly disliked high school boy, J. developed a passion for jazz or maybe for blackness, even though he was hesitant with black men. The pursuit of records took hold of him and he brought to it the methodical, dogmatic anxiety of his nature. The music seemed to cut into his flesh, leaving a sort of scar of longing never satisfied, almost a wound of feeling. Like all passions it was isolating because there was much he did not admire that others would, to his fury, press upon him. And then he always said that it could be distressing to listen to jazz when one was troubled or with the "wrong" person. At times he would think of giving it up altogether, so difficult was it to define, even for himself, what popular music and certain ways of doing it were all about. What was it? . . . the sea itself, or youth alone?

* * *

We lived there in the center of Manhattan, scorning the ups and downs, somehow believing the very placing of the hotel to be an overwhelming beneficence. No star was to be seen in the heavens, but the sky was always bright with the flicker of distant lights. No tree was to be seen, but as if by a miracle little heaps of twigs and blown leaves gathered in the gutters. To live in the obscuring jungle in the midst of things: close to—what? Within walking distance of all those places one never walked to.

But it was history, wasn't it? The acrimonious twilight fell into the hollows between the gray and red buildings. Inside, the hotel was a sort of underbrush, a swampy footing for the irregular. What a mark the old hotel dwellers leave on your own unsteady heart—their brooding inconsequences, their delusions and disappearances.

These people, and some had been there for years, lived as if in a house recently burglarized, wires cut, their world vandalized, their memory a lament of peculiar losses. It was as if they had robbed themselves, and that gave a certain cheerfulness. Do not imagine that in the reduction to the rented room they received nothing in return. They got a lot, I tell you. They were lifted by insolence above their forgotten loans, their surly arrears, their misspent matrimonies, their many debts which seemed to fall with relief into the wastebaskets where they would be picked up by the night men.

The Automat with its woeful, watery macaroni, its bready meat loaf, the cubicles of drying sandwiches; mud, glue and leather, from these textures you made your choice. The miseries of the deformed diners and their revolting habits; they were necessary, like a sewer, like the Bowery, Klein's, 14th Street. Every great city is a Lourdes where you hope to throw off your crutches but meanwhile must stumble along on them, hobbling under the protection of the shrine.

The Hotel Schuyler was more than a little sleazy and a great deal of sleazy life went on there. Its spotted rugs and walls were a challenge no effort could meet and the rootlessness hardened over everything, like a scab. Repetition—no one ever escapes it, and these poor people who were trying were the most trapped of all.

Midtown—look toward the east, toward many beautiful and bright things for sale. Turn the eyes westward—a nettling thicket of drunks, actors, gamblers, waiters, people who slept all day in their graying underwear and gave off a far from fresh odor when they dressed in their brown suits and brown snap-brim hats for the evening's inchoate activities. At that time these loosely connected persons had about them an air that was sometimes thick and dumb and yet passive; the faces on the streets had not yet frozen into an expression of danger and assault, of malice and fearlessness, the glaze of death in the daylight.

The small, futile shops around us explained how little we know of ourselves and how perplexing are our souvenirs and icons. Watch the strangers in the city, poor people, in a daze, making decisions, exchanging coins and bills for the incurious curiosities, the unexceptional novelties. Sixth Avenue lies buried in the drawers, bureaus, boxes, attics, and cellars of grandchildren. There, blackening, are the dead watches, the long, oval rings for the little finger, the smooth pieces of polished wood shaped into a long-chinned African head, the key rings of the

Empire State building. And there were little, blaring shops, narrow as a cell, open most of the night, where were sold old, scratched, worn-thin jazz and race records —Vocalion, Okeh, and Brunswick labels.

And the shifty jazz clubs on 52nd Street, with their large blow-ups of faces, instruments, and names. Little men, chewing on cigars, outside in the cold or the heat, calling out the names of performers, saying: Three Nights Only, or Last New York Appearance.

At the curb, getting out of a taxi, or at the White Rose Bar drinking, there "they" were, the great performers with their worn, brown faces, enigmatic in the early evening, their coughs, their split lips and yellow eyes; their clothes, crisp and bright and hard as the bone-fibered feathers of a bird.

And there she often was—the "bizarre deity," Billie Holiday.

Real people: nothing like your mother and father, nothing like those friends from long ago now living in the family house alone, with the silver and the pictures, a few new lamps and a new roof—set up at last, preparing to die.

At night in the cold winter moonlight, around 1943, the city pageantry was of a benign sort. Adolescents were sleeping and the threat was only in the landscape, aesthetic. Dirty slush in the gutters, a lost black overshoe, a pair of white panties, perhaps thrown from a passing car. Murderous dissipation went with the music, inseparable, skin and bone. And always her luminous self-destruction.

She was fat the first time we saw her, large, brilliantly beautiful, fat. She seemed for this moment that never again returned to be almost a matron, someone real and sensible who carried money to the bank, signed papers, had curtains made to match, dresses hung and shoes in pairs, gold and silver, black and white, ready. What a strange, betraying apparition that was, madness, because never was any woman less a wife or mother, less attached; not even a daughter could she easily appear to be. Little called to mind the pitiful sweetness of a young girl. No, she was glittering, somber and solitary, although of course never alone, never. Stately, sinister and determined.

The creamy lips, the oily eyelids, the violent perfume —and in her voice the tropical *l*'s and *r*'s. Her presence, her singing created a large, swelling anxiety. Long red fingernails and the sound of electrified guitars. Here was a woman who had never been a Christian.

To speak as part of the white audience of "knowing" this baroque and puzzling phantom is an immoderation and yet there are many persons who have little splinters of memory that seem to have been *personal*. At times they have remembered an exchange of some sort. And of course the lascivious gardenias, worn like a large, white, beautiful ear, the heavy laugh, marvelous teeth, and the splendid head, archaic, as if washed up from the Aegean. Sometimes she dyed her hair red and the curls lay flat against her skull, like dried blood.

Early in the week the clubs were *dead*, as they spoke of it. And the chill of failure everywhere, always visible in the cold eyes of the owners. These men, always changing, were weary with anxious calculations. They often held their ownership so briefly that one could scarcely believe the ink dry on the license. They started out with the embezzler's hope and moved swiftly to the bankrupt's torpor. The bartenders—thin, watchful, stubbornly crooked, resentful, silent thieves. Wandering soldiers, drunk and worried, musicians, and a few people, couples, looking into each other's eyes, as if they were safe.

My friend and I, peculiar and tense, experienced during the quiet nights a tainted joy. Then, showing our fidelity, it seemed that a sort of *motif* would reveal itself, that under the glaze ancient patterns from a lost world were to be discovered. The mind strains to recover the blank spaces in history and our pale, gray-green eyes looked into her swimming, dark, inconstant pools—and got back nothing.

In her presence on these bedraggled nights, nights when performers all over the world were smiling, dancing, or pretending to be a prince of antiquity, offering their acts to dead rooms, then it was impossible to escape the depths of her disbelief, to refuse the mean, horrible freedom of a savage suspicion of destiny. And yet the heart always drew back from the power of her will and its engagement with disaster. An inclination bred from punishing experiences compelled her to live gregariously and without affections.

Well, it's a life. And some always hung about, as there is always someone in the evening leaning against the monument in the park.

A genuine nihilism; genuine, look twice. Infatuated glances saying, Beautiful black star, can you love me? The answer: No.

Somehow she had retrieved from darkness the miracle of pure style. That was it. Only a fool imagined that it was necessary to love a man, love anyone, love life. Her own people, those around her, feared her. And perhaps even she was often ashamed of the heavy weight of her own spirit, one never tempted to the relief of sentimentality.

In my youth, at home in Kentucky, there was a dance place just outside of town called Joyland Park. In the summer the great bands arrived, Ellington, Louis Armstrong, Chick Webb, sometimes for a Friday and Saturday or merely for one night. When I speak of the great bands it must not be taken to mean that we thought of them as such. No, they were part of the summer nights and the hot dog stands, the fetid swimming pool heavy with chlorine, the screaming roller coaster, the old rain-splintered picnic tables, the broken iron swings. And the bands were also part of Southern drunkenness, couples drinking Coke and whiskey, vomiting, being unfaithful, lovelorn, frantic. The black musicians, with their cumbersome instruments, their tuxedos, were simply there to beat out time for the stumbling, cuddling fox-trotting of the period.

The band buses, parked in the field, the caravans in which they suffered the litter of cigarettes and bottles, the hot, streaking highways, all night, or resting for a few hours in the black quarters: the *via dolorosa* of show business. They arrived at last, nowhere, to audiences large and small, often, with us, depending not upon the musicians but upon the calendar of the park, the other occasions from which the crowd would spill over into the dance hall. Jimmie Lunceford's band? Don't they ever do a slow number?

At our high school dances in the winter, small, cheap local events. We had our curls, red taffeta dresses, satin shoes with their new dye fading in the rain puddles; and most of all we were dressed in our ferocious hope for popularity. This was a hot blanket, an airless tent; gasping, grinning, we stood anxious-eyed, next to the piano, hovering about Fats Waller, who had come from Cincinnati for the occasion. Requests, insolent glances, drunken teen-agers, nodding teacher-chaperones: these we offered to the music, looking upon it, I suppose, as something inevitable, effortlessly pushing up from the common soil.

On 52nd Street: Yeah, I remember your town, she said, without inflection.

And I remember her dog, Mister. She was one of those women who admired large, overwhelming, impressive dogs and who gave to them a care and courteous punctuality denied everything else. Several times we waited in panic for her in the bar of the Hotel Braddock in Harlem. At the Braddock, the porters took plates of meat for the dog to her room. Soon, one of her friends, appearing almost like a child, so easily broken were others by the powerful, energetic horrors of her life, one of those young people would take the great dog to the street. These animals, asleep in her dressing rooms, were like sculptured treasures, fit for the tomb of a queen.

The sheer enormity of her vices. The outrageousness of them. For the grand destruction one must be worthy. Her ruthless talent and the opulent devastation. Onto the heaviest addiction to heroin, she piled up the rocks of her tomb with a prodigiousness of Scotch and brandy. She was never at any hour of the day or night free of these consumptions, never except when she was asleep. And there did not seem to be any pleading need to quit, to modify. With cold anger she spoke of various cures that had been forced upon her and she would say, bearing down heavily, as sure of her rights as if she had been robbed: And I paid for it myself. Out of a term at the Federal Women's Prison in West Virginia she stepped, puffy from a diet of potatoes, onto the stage of Town Hall to pick up some money and start up again the very day of release.

Still, even in her case, authenticity was sometimes pushed aside. A vague stirring in her mind and for just a moment a stereotype burst through and hung there like a balloon over the head of the heroine in a cartoon. The little girl with her mop, clothes on the line, the wife at the stove, a plate or two, candles. An invitation for chili: *my turn.*

J. and I went up to a street in Harlem just as the winter sky was turning black. Darkened windows with thin bands of watchful light above the sills. Inside, the halls were dark and empty, filled only with the scent of dust. We, our faces bleached from the cold, in our thin coats, black gloves, had clinging to us the evangelical diffidence of bell-ringing members of a religious sect. Determination glacial, timid, and yet pedantic. Our frozen alarm and fascination carried us into the void of the dead old tenement. The house was under a police ban, partly boarded up with pieces of tin. A policeman gloomily stood guard near the stoop. When we whispered her name he stared at us with furious incredulity. She was hounded by the police, but for once the occasion was not hers. Somewhere, upstairs, behind another door, there had been a catastrophe.

Her own records played over and over on the turntable; everything else was quiet. All of her living places were temporary in the purest meaning of the term. But she filled even a black hotel room with a stinging, demonic weight. At the moment she was living with a trumpet player who was just becoming known and who soon after faded altogether. He was as thin as a stick, and his lovely, round, light face, with frightened, shiny, round eyes, looked like a sacrifice impaled upon the stalk of his neck. His younger brother came out of the bedroom. He stood before us, wavering between confusing possibilities. Tiny, skinny, perhaps in his twenties, the young man was engrossed in a blur of functions. He was a sort of hectic Hermes, working in Hades, now buying cigarettes, now darting back to the bedroom, now almost inaudible on the phone, ordering or disposing of something in a light, shaking voice.

Lady's a little behind. She's over-scheduled herself. Groans and coughs from the bedroom. In the peach-shaded lights, the wan rosiness of a beaten sofa was visible. A shell, still flushed from the birth of some crustacean, filled with cigarettes. A stocking on the floor. And the record player, on and on, with the bright lift of her songs. Smoke and perfume and somewhere a heart pounding.

One winter she wore a great lynx coat, and in it she moved, menacing and handsome as a Cossack, pacing about in the trap of her vitality. Quarrelsome dreams sometimes rushed through her speech and accounts of wounds she had inflicted with broken glass. And at the White Rose Bar, a thousand cigarettes punctuated her appearances, which, not only in their brilliance but in the fact of their taking place at all, had about them the aspect of magic. Waiting and waiting: that was what the pursuit of her was. One felt like an old carriage horse standing at the entrance, ready for the cold midnight race through the park. She was always behind a closed door—the fate of those addicted to whatever. And then at last she must come forward, emerge in powders and Vaseline, hair twisted with a curling iron, gloves of satin or silk jersey, flowers—the expensive martyrdom of the "entertainer."

At that time not many of her records were in print, and she was seldom heard on the radio because her voice did not accord with popular taste then. The appearances in nightclubs were a necessity. It was a burden to be there night after night, although not a burden to sing, once she had started, in her own way. She knew she could do it, that she had mastered it all, but why not ask the question: Is this all there is? Her work took on, gradually, a destructive cast, as it so often does with the greatly gifted who are doomed to repeat endlessly their own heights of inspiration.

She was late for her mother's funeral. At last she arrived, ferociously appropriate in a black turban. A number of jazz musicians were there. The late morning light fell mercilessly on their unsteady, night faces. In the daytime these people, all except her, had a furtive, suburban aspect, like family men who work the night shift. The marks of a fractured domesticity, signals of a real life that is itself almost a secret existence for the performer, were drifting about the little church, adding to the awkward unreality.

Her mother, Sadie Holiday, was short and sentimental, bewildered to be the bearer of such news to the world. She made efforts to *sneak* into Billie's life, but there was no place and no need for her. She was set up from time to time in small restaurants which she ran without any talent and failed in quickly. She never achieved the aim of her life, the professional dream, which was to be "Billie's dresser." The two women bore no resemblance, neither of face nor of body. The mother seemed to meet each day with the bald hopefulness of a baby and end each evening in a baffled little cry of disappointment. Sadie and Billie Holiday were a violation, a rift in the statistics of life. The great singer was one of those for whom the word *changeling* was invented. She shared the changeling's spectacular destiny and was acquainted with malevolent forces.

She lived to be forty-four; or should it better be said she died at forty-four. Of "enormous complications." Was it a long or a short life? The "highs" she sought with such concentration of course remained a mystery. I fault Jimmy for all that, someone said once in a taxi, naming her first husband, a fabulous Harlem club owner when she was young.

Once she came to see us in the Hotel Schuyler, accompanied by someone. We sat there in the neat squalor and there was nothing to do and nothing to say and she did not wish to eat. In the anxious gap, I felt the deepest melancholy in her black eyes. She died in misery from the erosions and poisons of her fervent, felonious narcotism. The police were at the hospital bedside, vigilant lest she, in a coma, manage a last chemical inner migration.

Her whole life had taken place in the dark. The spotlight shone down on the black, hushed circle in a café; the moon slowly slid through the clouds. Night—working, smiling, in makeup, in long, silky dresses, singing over and over, again and again. The aim of it all is just to be drifting off to sleep when the first rays of the sun's brightness begin to threaten the theatrical eyelids.

The star, the great person, seen in the night, does not mix in memory with your own shady history. J.—do you remember Lena, running the carpet sweeper at the hotel, she with her *blood*, Portuguese, Indian, and African. Was she one or three disastrously adrift souls? There she is mashing a banana in a small bowl and spreading the mash on a piece of bread. One day she arrives with manic, spendthrift energy and the next, sudden slumps and languors. Sometimes seeing her approaching on the street she walked like an Indian, slow and plain. Another day she arrived as wild and florid and thickly brilliant as a bird.

In the hotel lobby, tired bandsmen, dark glasses, ashen sleeplessness, oppressive overcoats, their wives, blond and tired. Tired creatures of the saxophone, the trumpet, basses; sweating booking agents lying in wait. The "vocalist" carrying a load of long dresses on her arm.

I knew well those in the old furnished rooms up around Columbia. They had about them a left-over, dim, vanquished aspect, depressed spirits living in a conquered territory. The discontent of the people at the Hotel Schuyler was quite different. Most of them were failures, but they lived elated by unreal hopes, ill-considered plans. They drank, they fought, they fornicated. They ran up bills, they lied and fought confusion with mild debaucheries. They were not poverty-stricken, just always a little "behind." Undomestic, restless, unreliable, changeable, disloyal. They were not spinsters, but divorcees, not bachelors but seedy *bons vivants*, deserters from family life, alimony, child-support, from loans long erased from memory. They drank for three days and sobered for three. People with union cards—acrobats, ballroom teams. That act was presented terrible, they would say about the current bill at Radio City Music Hall.

Tell me, is it true that a bad artist suffers as greatly as a good one? There were many performers at the Hotel Schuyler, but they gave no hint of suffering from the failure of their art. Perhaps the art had changed its name and came to their minds as something else—employment.

The sadness of the lost years of practice, the lessons, the exercises, the muscles stretched, the horn-blowing, tap-dancing, the swirling tango, the anguish of the violin. It is too much to think of. Even for these people the horror of mastery had been theirs. They seemed to be from the small towns of large states, such as New Jersey or northern Ohio. Their faces mirrored the bleak urban surface, the jangling provinciality of the old highway suburbs. Old age was unimaginable. When, whither? Perhaps, perhaps lovers would turn into widowers in the nick of time, somebody, somewhere would settle a little property on them. Why not? It was known to happen. Old rakes and "models"—after all, they were not clerks or filling station attendants or grocers. They were only those who wanted a good time, to have fun, to grow blowzy and paunchy in a vivacious, noisy company. The night clerks, rodents with red eyes, gray faces, men who had spent all their lives on the night shift, who greeted the morning as the time to pull down the blinds—how they envied the tenants, the lucky ones we never pass by in life without asking: what do they live on?

* * *

My friend, our *mariage blanc*—things went on for another year or so and then we parted. There was something of a divorce in our leave-taking. Quarrels, anger, and boredom, each with his character and that of the other.

J. suffered in his loves from seizures of optimism, a blighting frenzy quite unknown to me. A meeting, an attraction, aroused in him a rich, agitated possessiveness. He rushed into the future with the first glance, swept along by a need for connection that extended the moment before it had begun. He was one of those who look into new eyes and say: Now I am going to be happy.

And yet a day scarcely passed before a shadow, a reluctance fell into the space, a small or large difference, an imbalance. Alerted to rejection on the very heels of enthusiasm and hope, he would then have to retreat. He would become sardonic, taunting, clever, epigrammatic. How he suffered, sustained again and again only by the ferocious power of his habits, by a consuming discipline.

Transformations and miracles of the will were not beyond J. He was quite handsome, but also soft and rounded and as determined against sports as if he had been born with a handicap. But one year he began the re-creation of himself in a daily, horrible contest with barbells, push-ups, excruciating exercises. And slowly the neck thickened, the chest expanded, the muscles of the arms were visible. An appalling lifelong force had entered his being, leaving his self intact but accompanied always by this screaming, exercising twin, a twin who called out in the morning and again in the evening, calling for time, breath, pain, sweat. By enormous effort, he finally succeeded in looking like others.

J. left the hotel first, and into his room moved a call girl and her pimp. The girl was named Miss Chadwick and she was from the South. I heard this news with desperation. Complicity entwined us and her smile came back to me as if I were looking in a mirror. She showed me a picture of her little son. Where is he? Mama's raising him, she said. That was all. Goodbye.

Goodbye? I have left out my abortion, left out running from the pale, frightened doctors and their sallow, furious wives in the grimy, curtained offices on West End Avenue. What are you screaming for? I have not even touched you, the doctor said. His wife led me to the door, her hand as firmly and punitively on my arm as if she had been a detective making an arrest. Do not come back ever.

I ended up with a cheerful, never-lost-a-case black practitioner, who smoked a cigar throughout. When it was over he handed me his card. It was an advertisement for the funeral home he also operated. Can you believe it, darling? he said.

The Hotel Schuyler is gone now. Uncertain elevators, dusty "penthouse" suites, the greasy, smoking ovens of "housekeeping units," the lumpy armchairs—a distracted life, near the Harvard Club, *The New York Times*, the old Hotel Astor, the Algonquin, Brentano's. In the halls you would sometimes hear a baby crying—child of a transient—and it was a sound from another world. The irregular tenants were most pitiful when they received visits from relatives, from their ex-wives, their grown children. They walked about sheepishly then, as if they had met with an accident. Soon the disappointed sons and daughters left, wives went back home, and at the Schuyler, free once again, our people returned to their debaucheries, their bills, and that stain of life-giving paranoia—limited, intact—each one wore like a tattoo.

Part Four

THIS IS WHAT I saw yesterday morning through the tall, old artist-windows of my apartment. The bright morning sky that day had a rare blue and white fluffiness, as if a vacuum cleaner had raced across the heavens as a weekly, clarifying duty. It is hard to set nature apart in the city, and everything, inside and out, takes on the frame of a relentless house-keeping. Someone has let the coffee boil over; on this floor it must be. No sun from the north, only the pacifying light. There on 68th Street I see a modern church and the back view of warm red brick is a *bella vista* of sorts.

On the upper floor of the church a nursery school is held during the mornings for children up to the age of five. Pasted on the windows are cutouts of pink and green trees, red apples, and a blue boat, listing. The children had gone from one room to the other. In the vacated room I suddenly saw a little boy approach the opened window. On his face there were the signs of a deep concentration and hurry—the fixed, determined frown of someone older.

First he threw out a small yellow ball, a ball of the purest yellow like the color of the early forsythia then coming into bloom in Central Park. He turned back in a rush and once more his little hand pushed through the window, this time dropping a painted box. He is gone for a second and again the hand comes through the open space; this time a small book falls from his fingers. The yellow ball, the box, and the book landed on a large, flat ledge below. He is seen no more at the window, his destruction ended. The rain came down on the ledge in the afternoon, diluting the orange paint of the box. The little book blew about in the rustle of rain and wind, gathering moisture. Only the yellow ball remained the same, gleaming without change in its plastic brilliance.

This is what I heard in the evening. At the party everyone was intelligent and agreeable, but not particularly good-looking. No person of talent had brought along a new, beautiful, young girl, who being new and not knowing all the names would seem rude and superior, thus sending arrows of pain into the flesh of the older people who were known for something. Eyeglasses glimmered. Academics, like old barons of the Empire, coughed out their titles and universities and yet quickly the badges dimmed and their faces returned to the resignation brought on from too many lectures, and the docile, not-quite-interested smiles of students.

The host and hostess were of high intelligence and thus were, in turns, anxious, bored, and pleased. Their apartment in the West 80's was typical of the city—the home of a bright young couple, where the man is paying alimony. Young children visited on the weekends, sleeping in the workroom of either the wife or husband, whichever labored at home. Books and records and pictures, a few pieces of old furniture well cared for, a number of handsome rugs and pillows, large plants in the southern window. Copper pans, some old silver, glazed casseroles in the neat square of kitchen.

A woman said: You can't ask permission to leave someone. That's where he made his mistake.

And if the permission came he'd be furious.

Exhausting.

Divorces and separation—that is the way to get attention. Everyone examines his own state and some say: Strange, they were much happier than we are. There are streets in the East 90's where youngish couples on the wave of success buy town houses and do them over at great expense, uncovering old wood, taking off the stoop so that drunks cannot loiter, making a whole floor for the children to be quiet on. The strain and the cost and the house, a mausoleum with both names on it waiting for the dates to be filled in, drives the couple to separation. The streets are called Death Row.

Two women recently divorced came up to me with inquisitorial and serious frowns. Are you lonely? they asked.

Not always.

That's marvelous, the first one said, smiling. The second said, gravely: Terrific.

How pleasant the rooms were, how comforting the distresses of New Yorkers, their insomnias filled with words, their patient exegesis of surprising terrors. Divorce, abandonment, the unacceptable and the unattainable, ennui filled with action, sad, tumultuous middle-age years shaken by crashings, uprootings, coups, desperate renewals. Weaknesses discovered, hidden forces unmasked, predictions, what will last and what is doomed, what will start and what will end. Work and love; the idle imagining the pleasure of the working ones. Those who work and their quizzical frowns, which ask: When will something new come to me? After all I am a sort of success.

There was talk about poverty. Poverty is very big this year, someone said. Talk about a trip to Mexico, about a sabbatical, about a very sick person, about a novel liked and very much disliked, about someone who drank a lot, about people taking up painting in middle age (mostly rejected wives), about New York and New Haven, about the swiftest creature in nature, a cockroach.

I began to talk to a handsome woman in her early forties. She is Judith: very thin, with short brown hair very thick and curly and worn in the African style that imparts, at least to white faces, a look of almost alarming cheerfulness and health.

Judith is not a happy woman. But there is a certain happy radiance in her bad choices, a certain aesthetic appropriateness and order in her dirges. She is a connoisseur, with a brilliant white smile, teeth perhaps a shade too large for sadness, beautiful eyes, perfectly in character, eyes that sparkled as if ready to cry.

She has a Ph.D., a credential very agreeable and surprising, since her life was all about love and disillusionment, as if she had been a courtesan rather than a scholar. She was wearing black silk pants and a blouse of flowered chiffon. She sighed behind her smile, with the resignation of experience, the harem resignation. All of her news was bad and so her talk was punctuated with "of course" and "naturally."

Yes, I have someone, but he lives in California, naturally. Of course, you can't exactly call that *have*.

She began suddenly to speak of her son. A mess. Do you really want to hear? Right now, where is he? He's gone, signed himself out of the hospital and wouldn't stay at home. He's twenty-one. I got married very young, of course, of course. The father—what father?—I think he's in Florida. No, not in the picture—naturally. No money. I raised the boy by myself. My father helped a lot. These things cost a fortune. It's not to be believed.

Now? The boy's just sitting around, actually living with a couple, both psychiatrists, and it's supposed to be therapy. They hate me, naturally. When he was with me a few months ago it was a nightmare.

I call. I call him a lot but he won't talk to me. I wanted him to go to this good place in Connecticut. He went and just walked out . . . Yes, depressed mostly, but then churns up and goes wild too.

She smokes, drinks a glass of wine, eats a bit of cheese. Drugs? How can you ask? Of course. More like amphetamines than anything else. He looks awful, very thin, a skeleton . . . Almost mute, except when he's high and then he laughs a lot. His skin is a disaster, very pale, almost green . . . No, no, beautiful as a little boy. Not dumb either, naturally.

She lowers her eyes. This thing with him is never going to be over, never.

Judith was quiet, contemplating the ten plagues. Is she an Egyptian or an Israelite? Is she the carrier or receiver of plagues? What about the lovers in the room next to the crib? Does he look too much like his father? Does she want to be twenty again? How the poison passes from one person to another is not clear, but Judith has been accused more times than a numbers runner.

Already, in the early spring, she has a suntan, just the lightest brown on her skin. She would like to do something better, something sacramental perhaps, but instead there is only the solitary climb up to the roof, in a sweater, to turn her pale face to the sun.

Frenzy suddenly. What day is this? God, Thursday. I always call my son on Thursday night. The bitch shrink answers, and you would think I was a bill collector or a breather. Then the husband shrink comes on: Did you want something? Then the boy comes on and says nothing. Finally he says, sure, it's okay here.

She looks for her purse. Thursday night. They want me to forget, naturally. All three of them. But I can't forget. Then they will remember that I forgot.

She puts a black shawl over her seraglio costume and rushes out. At the door she offers her little, hesitant smile of bad luck. How pretty she is with her kinky head, her large, camera teeth and the diamond brooch of her Ph.D. Men have mistreated her, a mild mistreatment, as one would speak of a mild case of, say, bronchitis. She provokes it with her charming harem discontent, with her veils of bad luck through which her eyes glitter with a curious ironic hopefulness. Goodnight, Judith. Take a drink before the telephone call.

A woman's city, New York. The bag ladies sit in their rags, hugging their load of rubbish so closely it forms a part of their own bodies. Head, wrapped in an old piece of flannel, peers out from the rubbish of a spotted melon. Pitiful, swollen sores drip red next to the bag of tomatoes. One lady holds an empty perfume bottle with a knuckle on top of it indistinguishable from her finger. They and their rubbish a parasitic growth heavy with suffering; the broken glass screams, the broken veins weep; the toes ache along with the ache of the slashed boot.

Have mercy on them, someone. And mercy on Miss Cramer, my old neighbor who has now descended to a smaller place around the corner, down near the abandoned police station, among the damnation of emptying red-brick buildings waiting for the executioner.

Monday in winter. What has happened to you, Miss Cramer? It is December and Christmas is near. There is a reindeer in the window of the steaming Chinese laundry; there is a wreath of peppermint paper in the ferocious prostitute's window and a lighted tree has been in the hardware store since Thanksgiving.

What has happened to the impertinent music teacher, the failed mezzo, who used to receive her pupils with sonorous black looks, sizing them up as if they were a bundle of remaindered goods asking to be patched together for use?

Miss Cramer in winter in a dress of printed silk, soiled here and there with a new pattern of damage. She is wearing torn canvas shoes and no stockings to cover her bruised, discolored legs, nothing to help the poor naked ankles caked with barnacles of dirt. And recently she has been struck by a loss beyond bearing: her two black poodles. Rich, resplendent animals, of perfect breeding like herself, accustomed to a dozen kisses on their cold, black muzzles each morning.

When we first moved to 67th Street, I applauded her amazing automobile and imagined she was assisted in her driving by her appropriate English accent. In the early days of summer the car came out of storage for the drive to the season in the Catskills. Come and see Miss Cramer in her car, I would say to my husband.

And there she was in a mannish felt hat, the top of the twenty-five-year-old miracle down, she, impressive as the car's shining black hood with its foxlike nose of silver; she sitting on the tan, burnished leather. She went down toward Broadway, deftly twirling her hands and pointing her arms right and left in the now-arcane signals, receiving the admiration of the passers-by for her marvelous effort of conservation. She is leaving the grand old two-story apartment for the summer, abandoning without sentiment the crackling, insecure voices trying out "Dové sono," "Un bel di," and "The Last Rose of Summer."

She then had her aged mother with her, a tyrant of primitive snobbery who, as she grew older and older, went back to the grievances of ancient robberies, thieving char-women, malicious in-laws. The mother was like the old woman Herzen mentions in his memoirs, the one who could not forgive Napoleon for the premature death of her favorite cow in 1812.

On Christmas Eve Miss Cramer is wearing the same print dress and a short knit sweater. She is almost bare-foot in the canvas shreds. Poverty for the autocrat came like a bulldozer, gouging out her pretensions, her musical education, her trips to Bayreuth. The mother died, summers vanished, the voices were silent. Out of the apartment went the piano and the trash of two and a half decades, brilliant American, English, and European trash.

Miss Cramer moved down the street, and the move was a descent on the roller coaster, hair flying, trinkets ripped off the ears and the fingers, heart pounding and her head filled with a strange gust of air, which was never again released and seemed to be still blowing about behind the brow, rippling the dark eyelashes.

How are you, Miss Cramer?

Very well, thank you, she replies without smiling and yet in possession of the full, throaty voice.

Today she pauses at the end of the block where trucks and cabs and cars are flowing and raging with their horns. She approaches an appalling wreck of great individuality, a black woman who wanders in and out of the neighborhood, covers the streets with purposeful speed. No one has ever seen the black woman's mouth, since the whole lower part of her face is always bound tight with a sort of turban of woolen cloth. Fear of germs, disfigurement, or symbol of silence? She has three large bags of rubbish, larger than herself, which she carries without effort. Her dark purdah glance is strong and still as rock. She gets on the city bus without fare and sometimes so black is her glance the driver shrugs in panic and lets her pass.

She and Miss Cramer meet suddenly at the corner and both stop for a moment. The wind is so strong a beer bottle rolls in the gutter. They are both fearless and they gaze bitterly at each other with their terrible virginal inviolability, their sore purity. These are not cases, they do not fill out forms or wait for the mails. They are gladiators, creatures of the trenches, accustomed to the streets at night, to the toughness of weather, the pain of stones, and the itch of dirt. Mad strength, hideous endurance, hostility, nightmares, met for a few seconds at the corner but it seemed to me that there was no sign of recognition. The two women do not know what they look like, do not see their lives, and so they wander about in their dreadful freedom like old oxen left behind, totally un-provided for.

Part Five

DEAREST M.: I saw Alex A. on the street recently. He is still handsome. I suppose that is, with him, the first thing one thinks—that and the waving shadow, the shadow of his own self-reproach. Not quite liking himself, he whom everyone adores. I must say he was wearing a very good-looking raincoat and so the "presentation" isn't much altered. That's something, isn't it? But what is his intention? I mean the intention of his life.

That was a year ago. And now it is this year. It is time for cocktails. The moment for which all of New York works, lies, exercises, hurries, dresses.

New York—this is no city for poor people. Their presence ruins everything, everything. Dread—that is the noxious air around them. The rich in their pyramids have a nice time. All of the objects of eternity are at hand, lest they down the years need something remembered or forgotten. A broken heart. The pharaohs need not even go outdoors to pace about in their pain, looking in shop windows, buying things. No, they may sit at home in a depression, a square of fur warming their knees, mending all the while. Everyone dreams of a servant when the ego is bruised, the vanity affronted.

To Alex I said on the telephone: You cannot imagine how well I am set up, how comfortable I appear to be, although a pauper.

It is almost seven. Should Alex walk in the door as a type, a genre? Perhaps that effort is a mistake. What is wanted is history, the man in the raincoat, wearing the loops of his ideas, the buttons of his period. Some men define themselves by women although they appear to believe it is quite the opposite; to believe that it is *she*, rather than themselves, who is being filed away, tagged, named at last like a quivering cell under a microscope.

Back there, when I first came to New York, I observed that a number of intellectual men, radicals, had a way of finding rich women who loved them in the brave and risky way of Desdemona. A writer or painter or *philosophe* sailed into port and a well-to-do woman would call out, *Evviva Otello!* The women were not necessarily sparkling and lighthearted. More often an impressive, thick, downright strength of purpose went along with them, like an overcoat.

Perhaps a sort of perverse complacency led the lucky women to rescue a smart, sulky man, one whose ambitions and gifts were far from settled, whose intelligence was certain but whose destiny was a curling, warning question mark. Gifts, sad and defining, books read, ideas stored—all intact and battered by an inconstant will.

Envy is not the vice of the frozen intellectual. How can it seize the mind when boredom arrives before it, always ahead of time, ready? Boredom with the results of those who are always working and producing, failing or piling up money and reputation, boredom with the ordinary thoughts laid out in carefully chosen type, bound for the ages, with indexes, chapter headings, ordinary thoughts dressed in the same coats and hats as the complete works of Spinoza.

Time—that is something else. With the hesitant intellectual years fly by like a day; life is shortened by the yellowing incompletes. The "book"—a plaguing growth that does not itself grow, but attaches, hangs on, a tumorous companion made up of the deranged cells of learning, experience, thinking.

Sometimes the moneyed women with their artists and thinkers were like wives with their vigilant passion for the Soviet Union, the huge land mass that had long ago aroused in them the blood loyalty and tenderness felt for a first child. And what are a child's "few mistakes"?

The pathos of high projects that cannot be set aside because of the investment, the "good parts," the research, the files, the old outlines. Healthy enough on the tennis court, to be seen at the opera, the ballet, the mysterious invalids have their charm. They know something very well, perhaps too well.

In the evening, wine may revive the dead Ph.D. and

in the warmth the weed-choked garden of ambition and love seems to burst forth with thorny, brave little blossoms like those on an ancient, untended rosebush. It is like the song in the hymnal, one of the many B-flat offerings of consolation.

> The sun is sinking fast,
> The daylight dies;
> Let love awake and pay
> An evening sacrifice.

And yet the perennial, hardy hope cannot last out dinner. This is New York, with its graves next to its banks.

It is a Friday night, October 1973. Smog and closeness during the long afternoon. Earlier at the New York Jewish Guild for the Blind a vicious burglar alarm was somehow tripped into violent sound. On and on it rang, as if a thousand ambulances were screaming through the city, whistling, careening, warning on their mission of remedy. The alarm sounded without mercy for an hour. One began to imagine the blind, with their pale flesh, soft and misted with blue, trembling in the corridors. A thousand little white canes tapping in panic, dogs growling in their harnesses.

My plants are brought in from their southern kitchen windows to rest in pots in the living room. The stationary schefflera in its heavy tub stands in its permanent corner, like a cat that never goes out, year after year, living its entire life in a few rooms. ("The plant can stand periods of poor light—north or east window or even interior location.") The weeping greens of the city shine in the dark and survive in a great will to accommodate. There they are, everywhere, determined, hopeful, like the coolness of evenings in the desert.

I am alone here in New York, no longer a *we*. Years, decades even, passed. Then one is out of the commonest of plurals, out of the strange partnership that begins as a flat, empty plain and soon turns into a town of rooms and garages, little grocery stores in the pantry, dress shops in the closets, and a bank with your names printed together for the transaction of business.

I often think about bachelors. A life of pure decision, of thoughtful calculations, every inclination honored. They go about on their own, nicely accompanied in their singularity by the companion of possibility. For cannot any man, young or old, rich or poor, turn a few corners and bump into marriage?

Alex is coming for a drink; he has never married but whether he is a true bachelor or not is another matter. Henry James, unwed, and well known for dining out with a statistical fervor, made his decision early in life and was thereby free to pass sociable evenings, untroubled by the errors of the ambivalent and discontent who are always going out and yet forever asking what good it has done them. To be single and busy—nothing bad in that. Such people do much good.

The trim, conservative bachelor calls up a picture of neat clothes, shoes in wooden trees, mahogany desks with leather fittings and brass antique writing instruments; glasses and bottles and ice buckets, matching curtains and pillows chosen by decorators or women friends, striped materials on the sofa. Record collection dusted, alphabetical; a stale but tranquilizing symmetry—and certain absences, like the bathroom of a blind man, without mirrors.

Beethoven was not married, nor was Flaubert. Voltaire lived thirty years longer than his mistress, and Dr. Johnson thirty after Elizabeth. Both lived out life in a populated singleness. Good for them. More restful than the material-mad Goethe with Ulrike, Marianne, Christiane, Charlotte, Gretchen, Käthchen, Friederike, Lotte, Lili, Maximiliane, Bettina, and Minna.

Last week. A young man suddenly found that his own mother had been given to him as a present. He cried out in rage, saying: My mother has collapsed completely, collapsed. Do you hear, can you imagine what that means? Have you ever heard the sound of a body falling, falling on you? He swore, eyes furious, swore at his father for dying in upstate New York. The plot was explained. They, the parents, fought without ceasing, never got along well, not from the first. She hated nursing him, the half-nursing of someone half-sick. The mother's face had for years worn a planning look: the face had been thinking of trips alone, when the father was gone, of insurance policies, of interesting assets to examine of an afternoon. "A rich widow weeps with one eye and laughs with the other."

Death, however, arrived as a farce. In an instant, she announced herself as the broken partner of a splendid alliance, the frozen, demanding survivor of a warm past. The young man, with his blond hair and enraged eyes, suddenly became the disheartened, unwilling caretaker of the last half of a hallowed union upstate. He ground his teeth as he heard the hearse of love coming his way.

A lot of bachelors are "queer" and many lay claim to a spurious bisexuality based upon instances minimal in number . . . Alex is not queer. He is indolent, anxious, likes rich people and clever people of all sorts. He is a snob, a dandy, and a Marxist. Why should it be an objection that he is the things he has the talent to do rather than the summation of what he has finished? Remember his suffering, so like the suffering of achievement itself. Remember how terrible it is to be touched in youth by the wing of the Muse, the curse of it, lifelong.

A few facts. Alex worked at the Museum of Modern Art, wrote book reviews in his twenties, reviews in which many negatives caught the eye. He chose as his lifework a book about democratic architecture. He was from someplace, Akron, and he knew what it was like for Hart Crane to be writing letters back home to Ohio, to Cleveland and Chagrin Falls. For A.—University of Michigan and a bit of time here and there at Harvard and Columbia.

Absence of links and information. What does he live on? He lives on mimicry, mimicry of the style he would practice if he had more money.

Talent and style can set the teeth of the ungenerous on edge, and more people are scorned for rising above themselves than for living out their lives on a legacy. Alex seemed ahead of his time in one thing: a complicated and hesitant attitude to marriage. But he was not a pedant and so was able to combine the single state with long, difficult, confining periods of *more or less* living with one person, one who always assumed the claims of ownership that are the temptation of marriage. What he held in abeyance, what the legal bachelorhood represented, was his grail, his lingering, half-hearted vision of self-realization.

A good deal of Alexander's life had been assigned to women. Much of his time had gone into lovemaking. Tonight, October, is our second meeting after a number of years. The last time, a month ago, he had told me that for a long period in his life he made love every night. He sighed, remembering his discipline and fortitude.

I said: Well, I read in the *Times* yesterday about an old couple in their seventies who do it every day. They spoke of being ashamed to admit it to the social worker.

Vehemence from him: I hate old couples.

I met Alex long ago when I first came to New York. He was very handsome and a little depressed by nature, but anxious to please and in this pleasantness somewhat impersonal. For that reason he was doomed to more fornication than he wished. His handsomeness, of course, played its part in the doom of pleasure. Brown, flattering, disingenuous eyes; dark hair that early flecked with gray; sunken, lucky shallows in a large, bony face; shadows of masochism and indolence. His last name is Anderson— some Norwegian there, perhaps; old square-faced ancestors, slow-tongued, patient, pastoral, nothing like him.

To get back to "long ago." To yourself on winter nights freezing in a thin red coat, and then a little lamp and a glass of whiskey at the bedside. And the telephone ringing, always there monitoring, as if it were your mother and father with their outraged, punitive screams. You go like a thief to these assignations with someone who belongs to another, or at least does not belong to you, you go slipping into the dark, groping about, critically sighing. You go in like a thief and always leave or are left as the robbed, thinking to look for your fake diamond pin in its old box, check the liquor cabinet, open the window and demand from the fleeing one the return of your new radio.

I slept with Alex three times and remember each one perfectly. In all three he was agreeably intimidating, and intimidating in three ways. 1. The murmured bits of dialogue, snatched from the air, grammatical encrustations, drifting clauses, ellipses. *Isn't this kind of evening the best of all?* Or, *Usually I*. On and on in whispers: *better than* and *women who* and *one time*—small, dark, drifting comparisons. 2. A seizure of spiritual discontent and a grave asceticism, mournfully impugning. 3. Regretfulness, kindness, charitable good humor, apologies for the lateness of the hour. Where is your little red coat? Can I take you to a cab? Or: You'll never want to see me again . . . too late . . . too early . . . no cigarettes left.

I was honored when he allowed me to go to bed with him and dishonored when I felt my imaginative, anxious, exhausting efforts were not what he wanted. His handsomeness created anxiety in me; his snobbery was detailed and full of quirks, like that of people living in provincial capitals, or foreigners living in Florence or Cairo. Worst of all was my ambivalence over what I took to be the inauthenticity of his Marxism. In my heart I was weasellike, hungry, hunting with blazing eyes for innocent contradictions, given to predatory chewings on the difference between theory and practice. That is what I had brought from home in Kentucky to New York, this large bounty of polemicism, stored away behind light, limp Southern hair and not-quite-blue eyes.

In those years I did not care to enjoy sex, only to have it. That is what seeing Alex again on Fifth Avenue brought back to me—a youth of fascinated, passionless copulation. There they are, figures in a discolored blur, young men and not so young, the nice ones with automobiles, the dull ones full of suspicion and stinginess. By asking a thousand questions of many heavy souls, I did not learn much. You receive biographies interesting mainly for their coherence. So many are children who from the day of their birth are growing up to be their parents. Look at the voting records, inherited like flat feet.

Casanova: The great exhilaration to my spirits, greater than all my own pleasure, was the joy of giving pleasure to a woman.

Some reason to doubt the truth of that. Still, reversals and peculiarities fall down upon those too proud of their erotic life. Even sacrifice may be a novelty. Alex's vanity was, like that of the dubious Casanova at the falsifying moment of composition, trapped in the belief that he had a special power, or perhaps a special duty, to please women. Having more charm than money played its part. So love was a treadmill, like churchgoing, kept alive by respect for the community. Many have this evangelical view of lovemaking: There! I've done it once today and twice the day before yesterday.

Orgasms of twenty years ago leave no memory. Better to be handsome and leave, like Alex, the image of lean

Egyptian features, a sloping skull, and conversations about the inability of the ruling class to *imagine*, to *experience*.

I am waiting; he is late. Changes, gaps—the embarrassments of the lifeline. The important women in Alex's life have not been good-looking. He liked Yankee types, aggressively plain, prudent, mulish, in love with their fathers—the kind who do not spend too much of their principal and who, of course, have principles. Few women have their own money; thus his real loves were rare.

For this last woman, Sarah, Alex and his book on architecture were a sacred trust. And how he must have winced under the watchful care, the dowdy concern for this capital, the holding on to his literary investment as if it were a small tract of undeveloped land, in the family so to speak.

Something terrible had happened to him. I felt it as he came into the room. Yes, it was as if he had come down from a bitter defeat in the North. The snow had fallen on him; the ice had moved too close. No matter, romantic style, a sort of athleticism, does not slump and sag overnight, and so he brought a careful gift, chosen for himself and for me. Simple, inexpensive, flattering. A paperback: *Chapters of Erie* by Charles Francis and Henry Adams.

A slip of paper marked a page by Henry Adams on the New York gold conspiracy and he read out: "One of the earliest acts of the new rulers was precisely such as Balzac and Dumas might have predicted and delighted in. They established themselves in a palace . . . a huge building of white marble, not unlike a European palace, situated about two miles from the business quarter, and containing a large theatre or opera-house . . ."

Another teacher of women. You haven't read Gibbon? How is that possible, you with such fine legs?

Alex's thin, flat hand pressed mine and the last strains of male coquetry played out with noticeable effort. Elizabeth, Elizabeth. You never gave me a chance.

Oh, indeed.

He was in a rout, mutiny in his camp. Not marrying, keeping his "studio" for the crippled book on architecture, for love affairs, for definition of self—all destroyed by a sudden delinquency. Sarah had left him.

And not only that, he went on. It was scarcely a few weeks before she was married. You can elope like a junior miss, no matter how old you are, if you are not in need of a divorce.

His long alliance, fifteen years, with the nervous, insistent, infatuated woman from Philadelphia—Sarah, who believed in the sacred book and in the hollows of his Oriental face, who was possessive, dominating, and in her plain, stubborn concentration, like the concentration of someone bending over a dangerous machine, perhaps a little mad. She came upon simplicities the way others came upon debts, naturally—and so baked tedious home-made bread, cooked dim soups from fresh vegetables, and stitched up her dresses out of Pakistani bedspreads. Still there was something cheerful and blinkered about these reductions. They were character, like her clear smile, clear teeth and the way she had of taking an editor aside and saying, Give him a deadline, do you hear? That will do it.

You have grown a little beard, I said.
You see it is not true that one can't change.

And how meek he looked decorated by the gray tufts. Yes, of course, he had begun at last to look like a family man, like one who is half of a couple and carries hidden from the world all the arguments behind the neat public smiles of appreciation, who falls in panic from the height of accepted marital discontent and yet is pleased to find a pillow as he lands. Monogamy drifted about him—the scent of a hot iron on a shirt collar. A bourgeois, thinking of retirement, of planting trees, of storm windows, of tiresome journeys by car that are pleasant to remember. Odd that all of this clung to him just when he was at last a true bachelor.

Disgusting, he said. Only those women with money can violate the laws of probability. And no matter what they do it will make sense. It is either a regression or a rebirth.

Sarah had taken a trip to Philadelphia, on the train. Her story was short indeed. That was the grandeur of it. On the train she met an old friend of her parents—the revered parents. She met the friend, elderly, rich, careful, widowed. And what a glance of patient conservatism the old friend must have cast upon her history, her sacrifices, her inclination for service.

The splendid old gentleman, trim from his long daily walks, spare from the salt-free cuisine of his Irish maid, sprang forth at her with the call of blood, leapt at her throat with memories of the pack and the clan. How I adored your mother. It's a wonder there wasn't a scandal . . . Your father was a national treasure . . . Dogs remembered, old partners in many teams of tennis doubles, people dressed in white with long, thin legs like wading birds.

Sarah turned her love and attention to the old man *immediately*. What style, Alex was shouting. *Immediately* . . . You ask how she took my surprise? . . . Pure sullenness . . . leaden sulleness . . .

And why not, Alex? It is well known that women carry poison in their pockets. Did you expect a gun? A woman with a gun would be just another policeman. We fall in love with the convicts, remember that. Policemen marry girls from the neighborhood; high school looms over their unions, the first uniform is her prom dress and his black bow tie and white shirt. But the girls are thinking of poison, thinking of poison as the lights go out on the dresser where the revolver has been placed with care for the night. The black shoes, the fine, thick serge of the coat, shoulders and thighs of stallions. And policemen are usually shot down by someone out of shape, thin, thin, nothing but living bones. Remember that.

I was wrong not to marry the person I loved, he said, voice fading.

Insurgencies, insolvencies. Living in his loved studio, among the rubbish of unvarying leisure, amidst the sinking silences of independence.

In a way, I said, you really were married to Sarah.

His voice rose again. No, no. You are not making sense. It is not the substance but the form that matters. The license, the will . . . the property rights, income tax . . . the cousins, the funerals . . . the photographs!

Photographs of marriage. Records of blood, decisions, sacraments observed. In my apartment, around us, in the old fading red-pine chest, in the mahogany desk, in the Swedish desk too, in the fumed oak blanket chest, in manila envelopes marked "trip to Europe" are my own photographs, three hundred or more, that bear witness to form; pictures in the drawer, in the old box, photographs that make one his own ancestor. Of others I have cared about, cared for years—not a trace, not a fingerprint. As it should be. Those who leave nothing behind cannot be missed for long.

Alex facing the blank, the liquid history quickly drying up: Christ! The letters, the packets of letters from boarding school, from the old uncle on the boat to Vera Cruz in the nineties. Those are the things that count.

Outside the sorrowing autumn night and the wind rustling the curtains within. Another drink and courteously the conversation shifted briefly, dipping to the side, turning for a rest from the blazing highway, all the way across the country, that represented the delinquency of Sarah.

He could look back to the forties, to the anti-Stalinist radicals. How happy he had been then; in the old *Partisan Review* days, the night when Koestler first met and insulted Sidney Hook; when Sartre and the French discovered Russia long after "we" had felt the misery of the trials, the pacts, the Soviet camps. Alex had lived in history; that is, he had lived through T. S. Eliot, Kafka, John Donne, Henry James; through Maritain, Gilson, and Alger Hiss.

But he could not give much to the side trip and so, turning back, his eyes rapidly blinking, his mood lowering to reflection, to a more becoming melancholy, he spoke of the sadness of living alone.

Alone? Hadn't that been the point? Ah, Delacroix said

of Rousseau that he had never faced fire except at the kitchen range.

Old English wallpaper, carpets, Venetian mirrors, decorated vases, marble mantlepieces, buzzers under the rug around the dining-room table, needlepoint seats: Alex was making an inventory of Sarah's Philadelphia house before her mother died. Complaining that there wasn't an Eakins . . . Naturally not . . . They weren't smart enough for that.

On he went. I cannot tell you how badly Sarah and her man have behaved . . . The smugness, the cheapness . . . Terrible, terrible clichés. Everything supposed to be of value turned overnight into an item of indictment . . . My writing, my politics, my life, my friends . . . Now listen, listen carefully. She had the nerve to say that it was not him . . . him . . . not at all. Merely the occasion . . . yes, she's capable of that phrase . . . No, the thing with us had been for a long time, she said. Dead . . . What a lie.

Everyone says that. I wouldn't take it seriously.

He was getting drunk. Don't tell me what to take seriously. I will take what I please.

Their trips, their lacerating frugal trips to Venice, all so painful because of his expansiveness, his natural chic. July visits to the North Shore around Boston, her sister, very boring indeed. There again, handsome yawls swaying down at the pier and brutal economies up at the house.

Listen, Elizabeth, you have no idea how much money these people can get their hands on . . . They don't need to buy things . . . Their comfort is in having the money. And awful opinions—the works, let me tell you. These old Yankees put up a front, but the Bill of Rights doesn't mean a thing in the crunch. They like to make war as well as anyone else . . . I am a romantic. I thought they'd all be like the elder Henry James—good, eccentric. *The Secret of Swedenborg*, how about that? . . . Divine, natural humanity . . . Remember, *Under the shadow of the Boston State House* . . . No, the world up there is a desert.

Maybe Sarah didn't like your having other women . . . if you did.

If I did? Of course I did. But that isn't the point . . . The point is that my fatal type is a plain woman, somewhat stingy, not very interesting . . . but high-minded in a frugal way . . . And with her own money to be frugal with . . . Not a lot, just enough . . . Enough to make her appear in my dreams like some old loved school principal with the keys, the reports, generations of grades in her head.

Listen, listen, listen, he would beg, and I was thinking that it would pass in a few months, so useful and kind is a quick, devastating disappearance, irrevocable, leaving in the blast of the storm the first seed of amnesia.

Listen. It is the prudish power of these women that attracts me . . . Beautiful, like thick hair or fine eyes. And the truth is that I have had nothing but the bare necessities from their torpid dollars . . . The cries of pain over my imprudence . . . You wouldn't believe the thrift of their Christmas presents . . . A miner's children come out better . . . And yet in a funny way they don't know the value of money . . . They get the zeros mixed up. Twelve thousand for a house? Isn't that a lot of money?, they say . . . Maybe they think it is a hundred and twelve . . .

He is leaving. Suddenly, at the door, a smile drifted

through the darkness of his face. All the bones lit up and the melancholy eyes glittered.

It is pleasant to lay out the evidence.

Up north, in Vermont, I knew two lonely men, furious with abandonment, shivering with ill-luck. One was left by his wife after twenty-five years and the other, after forty years of marriage, outlived his wife. Black, still nights, early snow, empty roads and half the summer houses boarded up, the furniture in icy sheets, the pictures leaving their blank squares on the dead wall, the shades drawn on a sunny afternoon in September, the houses waiting for June, when someone will come to lift the shades again, like pushing back a stone from the mouth of a tomb.

For the men—horror of mistakes in location, living like beasts locked in a stable. The friend betrayed by life was as pitiful as a leper.

We moved here for cheapness, for space to work, to get away from teaching, for the children, the air, the view.

Tell me, G., what is the worst. The quiet?

No, the worst was her feeling that she had done nothing wrong. Nothing wrong . . .

Had she?

She had done a great wrong. Over a dozen people suffered. I and our three children . . . They are grown, gone away, but they mind, yes they mind . . . His wife and his four children . . . Did you hear? Four . . . My mother, her father . . . Her father was much too ill for this. He died from the devastation of our family . . . within a few months . . .

When I said to her, How do you propose to make a life on these corpses? She said, I can only try.

The man whose wife died, died just as they were making a new life, setting themselves in order. They had planned to go from the good to the better; they had retired to the loved summer house. With an improvident madness quite unlike their usual way, this couple, not knowing death was in the garden, raced after perfection. I would rather cook looking toward the south, she said, and so the kitchen was moved from the north. He fell in love with porches in the summer and determined that his heart's wish was to sit on the porch all winter, and so foundations were laid, great glass windows lay glistening on the lawn and were finally set in place, long evenings over catalogues produced a beautiful Swedish stove, and the splendid new porch changed the shape of the old house, making it and the couple new and daring and full of light.

They were not alone. All the retired people labored and labored for perfection. Additions, new wings, roofs sliced off, stairways turned around, bedrooms on the first floor, trees cut down, trees planted. Profoundly difficult renovations undertaken to make life easier. The children's inheritance was used up, but one day there would be the house, reshaped often out of childhood dreams and wounds of six decades ago.

And then the wife died, just when all was ready and in harmony.

The large, lonely house in the lovely, lonely northern town. The cold nights and the copper bottoms of the pans slowly losing their sheen. Nothing to smile about in the afternoons on the improvident sun porch. Bachelors again, in their depopulated settings, like large animals in their cages in the zoo, with the name of their species on the door.

* * *

Dearest M.: Let me bring you up to date on Alex. He actually got a job in a small college in Ohio. He is working! Is it possible? He has married a plain woman, a nurse, with a job in a hospital. Alex is radical again and has the beard of a terrorist. The students like him and the faculty does not. He lives in a dreadful house and mows the lawn—starting over, poor, *on time* as it were.

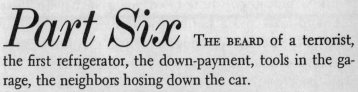

Part Six

THE BEARD of a terrorist, the first refrigerator, the down-payment, tools in the garage, the neighbors hosing down the car.

Dear old Alex: I will remember this for you.

I am eighteen years old and here they come, two people from the Communist Party in Cincinnati. The heat is full of dust, the grass is harsh and dry as straw, the dry roots of old flowers are gasping. That is the way it is. It is Sunday. Inside my house, around the dining-room table, there are more people than there are in the Communist Party in the state of Kentucky.

They, the two, have driven up in a gray-snouted car, a pitiful, abused drayhorse, loaded with newspapers and with pamphlets as frayed as last season's cabbage leaves.

The young woman and the older man are not attractive. They sit down on the porch swing, which moves back and forth on its old chains. Well, this is organizing the South, their tired, peculiar glance seems to say.

They handed me a Browder pamphlet. Popular front period. *Communism Is Twentieth-Century Americanism.* An interesting idea, she says.

I said: I have that in my room upstairs.

Good for you.

They sighed, lost in the downtrodden Sunday air. Are there any *good* people in Lexington? they want to know. Sighing again, listening to the questioning coughs and growls from the Sunday table, they soon leave on their dusty journeys.

Good people? There are some on High Street perhaps. A deteriorating old avenue, running east and west, its history sinking and rising. Nearby are the fraternity houses: whiskey, predatory, vacant-faced young men with their pins and rings and a terrible memory of their drunken singing, their drunken hands on my own drunken breasts.

A transcendental family lived on High Street. They were poor as their ancestors before them, never once brushed by the wing of comfort and savings, never once even on the middle of the ladder, teetering there hopefully. Instead they lived in a dreaming world of ideas which had come to them almost like a missent letter or one of those messages in a bottle that float on currents continents away. The family had learned about Soviet communism and experienced the multifarious tremblings of conversion.

The house—who knows who once owned it or owned it then? It had few of the seams and patches of proprietorship, none of those expanding arms grown over the years. It was painted in the unhappy two tones of tan and brown much in favor at the time. Winter showed the rotting porch of splintered wood against which the canvas summer chairs were propped. This was not, then, their own house, but at one time they were all in it: three generations, old parents, sons and daughters and grandchildren. They were mountain people, perhaps Scotch-Irish descendants of an emigrating crofter.

The father was tall and thin, with thick, straight hair the color of sand. The mother had an abashed and kindly manner, a sparsely fleshed Anglo-Saxon toothless jaw. Her solemn gaze and ruined smile sent forth its message: Appalachia.

The hero of the house was an ill son who lived, skinny and feverish, in an agitated convalescence brightened by passionate ideology. Inside the house in the chill of February, a warm, numbing air of gas stoves seemed to heat the brain more than the bones.

The son lay under a mound of worn blankets, his lively, alert skull, his large ears pressing forward to life against the downward surge of his ill body. He lay under the quilts and under a blanket of papers, as if the old *Daily Workers* could give the body warmth, like rags. Pamphlets and boxes and sacred texts surrounded him, the accumulation of what he referred to, in a singsong rural speech, as "International Communism."

No doubt the son looked older than he was. He may have been twenty-one or thirty-one. He had thrown himself into a grand engagement, a bizarre far-flung battle that reached out from an arsenal of strange sounds, the peculiarly pronounced but well-understood mottoes of Marxist-Leninism, the slogans of party belief. The names of European communists, of Togliatti and Thorez, enshrined home figures like Mother Bloor, the reviewers, writers and propagandists of *The New Masses*—an extraordinary oratorio, high notes and low, poured forth from the head jutting out of the covers. Dictatorship of the proletariat, the masses, the ruling class, the *lumpen*, the vanguard.

Sometimes, when his health was better, he might be seen hobbling down High Street to Main, rushing on to the great cathedral, the Post Office, the giver and receiver of life. Mail, papers, reports, rebuttals, accusations and counteraccusations, denunciations and affirmations: in this whirlpool he swam.

Confessions, executions and trials, bad news, came to the son, whose name was Lyle, as news in small print, not the main story. They might have been a long table of figures at the end of a thesis, or footnotes for a specialist. Here he was, a provincial acolyte, and what went on in the vague and thrilling transformed land came to him as murmurings of misrepresentation, bias reported by enemies. Turning pale, his throat a quivering rope, in a dejection of mind but never without hope, the son struggled for sanity. Poor young man. No one knew him and he knew no one, no one in the news, not one of the names so richly near to his thoughts. No policeman sought him out and only the mailman wondered about him.

The frenzy of politics in the battered house, the obscure discussions in the high mountain accents, the knowledge in the yellowing newsprint, surplus value, superstructure. Into the place of love and ambition, of envy and pride there had grown instead the most consuming of the passions, politics, to fill every cell of being.

So far as I know, the family has gone. How can you tell about people who have never been in the phone book? Sometimes they disappear, as into a collapsing mine shaft. Off some place or back to some place. Black people moved into the tan-and-brown house. New themes to mingle with the dust of the old ones.

*   *   *

Lyle was friendly with another native "red" who had the look of a clever turkey. This friend, an isolated, gawky gnostic, always rolling cigarettes, weak-chested and yet energetic, was mysterious. There was something quarrelsome about him although he did not quarrel; it was perhaps that one felt he was engaged in a silent disputation in his head. With his long gobbler's neck, his little mustache, his lidded turkey eyes, he looked like a small-town detective and yet he was the opposite of that. He himself was the one most likely to feel a hand on his wrist and an official voice saying: Come with me. He talked very little, but with a funny nicotine grin he would say that he had been born in October 1917. Under the very star and sign of the Revolution. Born in Ohio, just over the border.

For a time he had a small office, a shack near the old railroad station. There he ran off sheets on a mimeograph machine, sheets which announced meetings few attended except for an occasional troublemaker, the contentious radical university students who were Socialists or Trotskyites. Ruthlessly they attacked Mason—that was his name, first or last—and the blur of his cigarette eyes thickened almost to blindness.

Mason at least knew one pure, perfect joy. That was to go to the polling station near the courthouse and to write in the names of Communist Party candidates on election day.

Marie, Marie, in your cloudy eyes there is the same misty defense against apostasy that recalls to me Mason in his stubborn cigarette clouds. Marie was much later, a rich young woman who spoke in a drifting voice of Building Socialism. Socialism appealed to her as a more pleasant word than communism, or perhaps there was a flutter of prudence in the preference.

Marie was timid and reserved. She had been to the best schools and yet was ill-educated because she read mostly polemical left-wing magazines, pamphlets, and appeals for funds. These rags comforted her in the cold just as they warmed the shallow bed for Lyle. A modest structuralism unites the obscure, worn-out, skin-and-bones ideologist I remember from the shabby, penurious back streets of home and the industrialist's daughter who lived for a time on Central Park West.

Marie adored her parents and these lucky, conventional people seemed to accompany her wayward thoughts like agreeable escorts, one on each arm. On the coffee table in her bare apartment, there were sycophantic histories bound in leather about the founder of the family fortune. She knew every detail of her family's sudden, clever leaps to prosperity; she was interested in their travels, in cottages in the British Isles where perhaps some unrecorded ancestor might have been born, in villages where there were simple folk with her own name.

In her white bedroom, next to the pure white bed that seemed to promise a rest under a mist of snowflakes, there was the wedding photograph of her parents, smiling down from a silver frame studded with amethysts. Mostly, Marie lived with her own curiously compelled deprivation, like a contemplative without the athletic vigor required for the consumption of cars, flowers and pictures, winter houses and summer houses, plates and tablecloths, batik and baskets, little things with their miracles of microscopic inlay or big, bold almost hideous wonders.

With Marie, the slumps and gaps, the holes and blanks

were troubling, like a stutter. She gave away large sums of money, but in encounters with the working world she was meticulous and even stingy. A waiting hand received from her the boldest rebuke. Waiters, cab drivers and delivery boys saw her nickels and dimes and watched her disappear like a ghost.

Somewhere in her life a talisman had appeared. It might have come to her in a dream, this talisman which was a word: Russia.

For a time she had a lover, Bernie. He was terrible to look at. Very short, and if not fat, with too many muscles and bulges. Bernie was put together like a pumpkin, or two pumpkins, one placed on top of the other. The top was his merry, jack-o'-lantern face with its broken teeth.

Bernie spoke of bad news in a happy, growling voice, cheerfully predicting the fall of things or the ominous rise of things if the fall did not take place. Calumnies, falsehoods in the press, prejudices rooted like carrots in history: all of this bubbled and flowed from him like the song of a boatman:

> O heavenly delight
> to brave the tempest
> with a manly breast.

Often during his political singing of disasters Bernie smoked a cigar or nibbled from a packet of peanuts in his pocket. Bernie had the answer to every question except that of Marie. She had known so many kisses and compliments in youth. So, there was power in her thin wrists, in her long, slender fingers polished in an ivory color, power even in her slight, fastidious appetites so different from his own hungers.

Seeing Bernie come out of the bedroom, pulling at his shoelaces, was a shock. The bed was so white and small; the bottles and pencils, the pale-blue glass objects lined up by the window were not welcoming to a man's presence. His blue workshirts, his large hands, the glee of his growlings filled the space in the apartment as if he had brought with him a lot of old trunks.

What was Marie thinking of? Coups d'état, crowds in the streets with fists held high, banners asking for bread and land, straggling armies from the north, guerrillas in the mountains?

Perhaps her dreams are of a more domestic shape. She is thinking of petitions, of contributions, of revolutionary schoolchildren with round, well-fed faces singing songs, of calisthenics in the squares, of collective farms, workers' councils, housing developments, women doctors, and birth control.

Still, with a steadiness like nothing so much as that of a bird hovering outside the nest of its young, she maintained in balance her first flights. Faraway countries were caught in the arms of her timeless approbation.

Marie, I do not understand your fear of disillusion. Don't you see that revision can enter the heart like a new love?

After such conversations she would send a clipping from the communist press, explaining or denouncing criticism. At the top of the clipping in her neat handwriting: I thought this might interest you, dear friend. With love, Marie.

* * *

Her match with Bernie was a deprivation for him and he was discovered to have a mistress, a militant, sexy, talkative comrade. Marie was surprised and wounded and remembered that even her father had admired Bernie's intelligence. She was left with her grave, immobile fervor.

In the sixties we saw Marie in Italy, in Florence, where she had been as a girl to meet the past without pain, to flower like a fuschia or a gardenia in the mist of paintings and churches. But Marie had no interest at all in paintings, in the structure of churches, in the true difficulties of music and poetry. She did not know this, since she had been well brought up. A calm philistinism, courteous and unpolemical, was deeply rooted in her spirit and gave the clue—or part of it—to her wincing confusion about the claims of all those oddly named writers, poets, and painters imprisoned or killed. This was not callousness; it was blankness, a blankness without meanness such as one finds sometimes in priests and nuns.

In Florence there was a young Italian often in her apartment. He had thick wavy hair, bad teeth, an uningratiating manner, sometimes dignified, sometimes absent. His name was Benito and he had a sister named Edda.

Benito worked at a shoe store behind the Arno, and that had been the scene of their meeting. Sometimes on a slow day he stands at the window and his imperturbable face catches the eye. He may live far from the center, but one does not imagine that he would go home in the afternoon to eat or to sleep. Instead he is more likely to spend the time kicking a football in the park.

Benito brought with him wherever he went a large companion, a German shepherd. At Marie's house most of his attention went to the dog, to giving it high-voiced instructions, to gazing into the animal's excited eyes. While we talked English he talked to the dog.

Nothing new with Marie. The money holds, even grows, in the historical soil. Revelations of her college years, more than twenty years ago, hang on, subdued but flickering still. It is restful and yet puzzling. Nothing seems to happen. Armies gather with their unpleasant news, ossification sets in even though there is great activity everywhere. Sometimes she appears to be thinking there has been a miscalculation in the political universe. Dragons with seven heads and ten horns: were they not seen this year? A leopard came out of the sea and sank back down. But patience, patience.

Part Seven LAST YEAR a large
new office building began to go up on my small, narrow
street in New York. It is an odd street, filled with old
apartment houses of modest size which were built just
after the turn of the century for the accommodation of
artists. "Des Artistes," as one of the buildings is named,
were to work and live in the same quarters, to paint in
their ateliers like Frenchmen with little pointed beards,
and to eat in their dining rooms off the kitchen like
Americans.

The large windows of the studio room were then covered with opaque glass, according with the theoretical
beliefs of the time. The light was dimmed—to free the
mind for the light of the imagination? A northern smooth-
ness and easels upon which stood half-finished portraits
waiting for the sitter or the model, a colorful old man
or a loosely draped girl, or still lifes from the fruit bin.

I have seen several paintings done here in the house

long ago in the grayed daylight. One took as its subject a picnic in the Bois de Boulogne in Paris. The women were wearing fashionable clothes of the 1920's. All was sunlight, flowers and trees and dresses with mauve ribbons.

The thick glass is gone from most of the windows, but now a new building roars up across the street, arriving with a hideous grinding. Exquisite machinery stands about all day and night, and the steel skeleton with its artful modernity is more fit to decorate the city scene than the new building itself. The noise of construction will one day die down, and yet the light will never return to the artist-building. It is back in its glassy opacity. Perhaps some sort of preservation is taking place.

The Bois de Boulogne, the picnics, the apples and oranges on tables covered with paisley shawls, agreeable memories recorded in twilight: it is just as well the old painters have slipped away, leaving the space to be occupied by the brilliant electric glow of more recent tenants, the photographers.

It has happened that someone I do not know is staying in the apartment with me. One of those charitable actions insisted upon by a friend. The stranger, thin as the elegant crane outside the window, casts a shadow because she has arrived when I was thinking about the transformations of memory. She fills the space with both the old and the new twilight, the space reserved for thoughts of my mother. My mother, whom I lived very close to for more than thirty years, is this morning dimmer to me than this friend of a friend.

Louisa spends the entire day in a blue, limpid boredom. The caressing sting of it appears to be, for her, like the pleasure of lemon, or the coldness of salt water. A striking stasis can be seen in her eyes, nice, empty, withdrawn and staring eyes—orbs in a porcelain head. At such moments she looks her best, very quiet, her face harmoniously fixed, as if for a camera to which these rooms are now appropriate. My brown, skinny cat stares at her, with a yellowish Oriental gaze much like her own. They often look deeply at each other, but it is a look without seeing, just like two mirrors exactly placed on opposite walls. This morning, her second here, she watched the cat fall asleep, his lids suddenly closing, tightly, quickly, strangely calling upon the operations of a mysterious brain. She said, They can sit for hours, years in front of the television set, but they don't see it. I cannot understand how it is that nothing changes them.

Then she would take a cigarette out of the pocket of her smock, a bright piece of colored silk she put on in the morning and changed into immediately after returning from her excursions into the streets. She drew on cigarettes as if they were opium, an addition to the opium within her, the narcotic of her boredom, that large, friendly intimate, so dear and faithful. An immaculate drug the boredom seemed to be, with its hazy drift of dreams, its passivity pure and rich as cream.

After a dreamy day, Louisa went into her nights. Always she insisted they were full of agitation, restlessness, torment. She was forever like one watched over by wakefulness in her deepest sleep. She awoke with a tremor in her hands, declaring the pains, the indescribable, absorbing drama of sleeplessness. The tossing, the racing, the battles; the captures and escapes hidden behind her shaking eyelids. No one was more skillful than she in the confessions of an insomniac. These were redundant but stirring epics, profoundly felt and there to be pressed upon each morning, in the way one presses a bruise to experience over and over the pain of it.

Her hypnotic narration is like that of some folk poet, steeped, as they say, "in the oral tradition." Finally, it goes, sleep came over me . . . At last . . . It was drawing near to four o'clock. The first color was in the sky . . . Only to wake up suddenly, completely.

Unsavory egotism? No, mere hope of definition, description, documentation. The chart of life must be brought up to date every morning: Patient slept fitfully, complained of the stitches in the incision. Alarming persistence of the very symptoms for which the operation was performed. Perhaps it is only the classical aching of the stump.

She will be leaving soon, the intruder, the dramatic star of ennui with catlike eyes. She has come with no more force than a hand offering a delivery at the door. All the time she has been in the house I was planning to think of my mother. *To think*, that is to wonder what I would be forgiven for remembering or imagining. What do those of my flesh and blood deem suitable, not a betrayal? Why didn't you change your name? Then you could make up anything you like, without it seeming to be true when all of it is not. I do not know the answer.

My father, for instance. He is *out*, because I can see him only as a character in literature, already recorded. I will say, can say, he was very handsome, and indeed, when embalmed, with his hair parted on the wrong side, his profile reminded everyone of that of John Barrymore. He was not well educated, but very intelligent and read a great many true detective magazines and newspapers.

He sang beautifully and knew all the verses of many, many songs. He worked as a laborer and as little as possible. As a plumber, as a seller of furnaces, as something in the health department at the courthouse, as something in the Democratic party machine. He was not defined by work but by the avoidance of it to leave time for other things; for gossip, for card-playing at the firehouse, for football games, for going to bed and creating children, for smoking cigarettes, for frying bacon, for going fishing. He was political, and he and I got up early in the morning to listen on the radio to the fall of Madrid, the signing of the Munich Pact. We held hands and wept.

Sometimes when I am up in Maine and the men come to fix things—handsome, attractive people that they are, coming to fix a pipe, to measure, to take apart a motor, to drag a car to the garage—often then I find myself falling into a flirtatiousness, a sort of love for their *look*, their sunburned faces, their fine oiled workshoes, their way at the wheel of a truck, their jokes about the bill, their ways with other men, downtown drinking coffee, or inside a house under construction, or at the ravaged shed of the boatbuilder, their strong fingers yellowed from nicotine.

Then I think of my father, of Papa, and wonder what it would be like to be married to such a man, to see him coming out of the shower, to sit at dinner at six o'clock, turn off the lights at nine, embrace, make love frequently in honor of a long day of working, get up at five, visit with the relations on Sunday, never leave town.

I wonder about this and of course I know. I know what the men are like, but I do not know what she is like, she with her washing of clothes, her baking, her dangling shutter never mended by the husband-carpenter, the broken lamp never fixed by the household electrician, the flowerless, shrubless plot of land of the town gardener. A mystery, but then one does not come home to start work again.

The writer is one of the first-born of the sons of the State of Tennessee. If this seniority brings with it none of the rights of primogeniture, it certainly has imposed the duty of filial veneration and regard for the land of his nativity.

> From *The Annals of Tennessee to the End of the Eighteenth Century*
> by J. G. M. Ramsey, A.M., M.D., 1853

My mother had in many ways the nature of an exile, although her wanderings and displacements had been only in North Carolina, Tennessee, Virginia, and Kentucky. I never knew anyone so little interested in memory, in ancestors, in records, in sweetened back-glancing sceneries, little adornments of pride. Sometimes she would mention with a puzzled frown *The Annals of Tennessee*, by her grandfather with the same name, but she had never read it. Ramsey, this curious son of Tennessee, lived where she also was born in Mecklenberg County, North Carolina, the place of the "widely regarded as spurious" Mecklenberg Declaration of Independence of May 1775.

She must have had a youth and she had those brothers and sisters whose names we bear. She spoke of one brother who had been "very smart," but that too came to a hazy end.

This brother, out of the blue, began to write letters to my mother. They arrived, unfortunately, from a mental hospital in upstate New York. They were extraordinary for their outstandingly beautiful handwriting. These calligraphic marvels, with every letter perfectly formed and set in very straight, evenly spaced lines, were written with a fine black pen. The content was coherent, the spelling flawless and the subject matter a sort of oratory. He liked to write letters on our national holidays, moments which provoked an intense patriotic emotion in him.

Dearest Sister Mary: On this splendid Fourth of July a brilliant sun is shining, as indeed it should shine to honor the heroic War of Independence in which our beloved nation fought itself free of foreign domination. No true American would slight the hazardous, God-protected journey of the Mayflower and the sweetness of the Pilgrims kneeling in their simple attire to give thanks at Plymouth Rock. Yet, the moment of Independence was the true flowering of our great country as it stepped forth to its hallowed future.

I must add that, if you wish to write me, I have not been known for some years as Robert Ramsey, but as Robert Douglas.

Yours in family love,
Robert Douglas

What a beautiful letter, my mother said. I don't see how Robbie could be crazy. He certainly wasn't when he saw my sister about ten years ago and by that time he must have been forty-five.

We wrote the director of the hospital and after a month or so received an answer about Robert Douglas, an answer which had none of the patient's grand flourishes. The director didn't seem to know much about my mother's brother, but said that he was in a "more or less calm phase."

A few years later we received a notice of his death and a request for burial fees. So, with fifty dollars, Robert Douglas was buried someplace. Somehow we learned that his change of name was not madness but the sensible urging of practicality that followed a period of financial stress, if *stress* is the accurate word.

The house is dark. Now all the children are born and she is in one bed, he in another, according to the custom of that time and "class." They do not know that couples who have no children, or one or two, pride themselves on remaining in one bed, the *matrimoniale*, until they are separated by some illness of old age.

My father is in the room next to the attic, reading and smoking. He may be a little drunk—it is night. She is pulling the blankets over her arms, watching the light from the moon filter through the flowered curtains. The years do not seem real: the numbers are merely words, five years, ten years, forty. They might be nouns—house, street, garage.

I do not believe they are thinking of lost youth. I do not believe they are afraid of death. I doubt whether they are wondering if they love each other or whether they are happy. It does not seem accurate to call this, whatever it is, one or the other. Nevertheless they are alive, full of opinions, of distastes, *ideas*, even. Anyway the night is good because it leads to the day, to shoes and stockings, to coffee, to drudgery and repetition, especially for her who perhaps looks forward to getting it done.

* * *

My mother was born in the 1880's, and the girl who visited here for a few days was born in the 1950's. Seventy years are nothing. The two women are not alike and neither represents her time or type. I would not defame the girl for her narcissism nor would I make too much of my mother's dreadful labors, labors laid to rest long ago.

Her children loved the races. Jack, my brother, was taken sick at the Louisville track and died soon after in his room in the Brown Hotel. Tommy died in his truck on the way to the horse barns. He was rushing to see the morning workout. Horses, noble antiques, have died badly too. The great horse Hambletonian ran at Newmarket in 1799 against Diamond for a bet of three thousand guineas. Hambletonian won but never raced again. Both animals had been violently "whipped and spurred by their jockeys."

Actually Louisa, the young girl visitor, has just gotten quite a good job. She knows a few things and a few people. She went out early, but not too early, in black pants and a black leather coat. She put on a scarf with the name of a French designer displayed with such prominence it might have been he who was the applicant.

She spoke to someone of having been to college, spoke of typing, of odd *experience,* meaning only previous work. She said untruthfully that she could certainly take dictation. They put her in a room and turned on a machine. When it went too fast for her rapid longhand, she stopped the machine and played the difficult part once more. Her typed-up dictation was well received.

She will not do too much nor too little and this is what

is wanted. She will have an apartment, a lover, will take a few drugs, will listen to the phonograph, buy clothes, and something will happen. Perhaps it will be good—or at least what she likes.

Part Eight

THE TRAVELS of youth, the cheapness of things and one's intrepid poverty. "All ye who love the Prince of Orange take heart and follow me."

So, it was Holland that year, 1951. Descartes, almost three hundred years before, had spoken of himself as the only foreigner in Amsterdam not on business.

An unfashionable *gracht* in the center of Amsterdam—the Nicolaas Witsenkade. A busy, bourgeois street bordering on sloppy waters and the towers of the Rijksmuseum in view toward the west. Houses with stone steps and made of yellow or red brick are lined up in a businesslike, practical, 1920's decency and dullness. Autumnal tile decorations on the facades and here and there fans of purple and amber glass over the doorways.

Housewives of centuries have created the pleasantly stuffy little rooms with their dark paneling, have hung round lamps, with shades of old tasseled silk, over the carpeted dining tables. The house is not handsome and the landlady worries about the apartment because it has been her own and everything in it is dear to her. Anyway we said as we met her anxious glance: What a triumph every country is.

He observed that the coziness of small countries could not always be expropriated by an invader.

Yes, a squat, round, shiny black stove that had worked for years with the solemn obedience of an old donkey tormented our days and nights with its balky resentment of a new and ignorant hand. Perplexing dying of the embers so soon after they had been coaxed to blaze. We crept into the cold sheets under the ancient thick coverlets and were held at head and foot by the heavy frame of the bed, pierced by the sharp metal of carved leaves and fruits, acute reminders of spring. Daylight came in a rush and the whole town came alive at dawn. The baker and coalseller arrived with such swiftness they might have been dressed and waiting throughout the night. Greedy travelers, Americans, hail the dawn of a new experience!

In the winter sleet blew through the beautiful town, graying the waters of the Amstel. In the spring, in daylight and in the early evening, we used to watch, on the porch that faced us, the life of the unemployed Indonesians. Their ancestors had been exiles, once flung out from the swamps of the Zuider Zee to the humid airs of Jakarta. Now their children were returned *colons*, geographical curiosities, back once more to the sluices and polders of home, the unfamiliar homeland that received them with the chagrin proper to what they were: a delayed bill, finally arriving.

The Indonesians gathered on their porch, sitting there as a disconsolate testament to the great energy of the Dutch, to old map makers, shipbuilders, moneylenders, diamond cutters, receivers of Jews, Huguenots, Puritans. The unions we were staring at had taken place on unimaginable sugar plantations, in the deranging heat of exhausting empires. Beautiful, liquid-brown women, silky petite mother-in-law, dust-colored child, their little wrists and ankles delicate as chicken bones. And the heavy, dry, freckled, tufted Dutchmen, homely and reassuring.

The disasters of the war still lay over the country, and yet all of our Dutch friends were reading Valéry Larbaud's *A. O. Barnabooth, His Diary*, enjoying the sly chic of the fabulously rich hero and his addiction to "boutiqueism."

The crowds of Amsterdam and even the countryside filled with people in their houses, each one a sort of declassed nobleman sharing the space as a tree would patiently accept the nightly roosting of flocks and flocks of starlings. All the knowledge of Europe seems to be nesting there, too. And a certain sadness, a gasping for breath. No, no, the strain is nothing. Take no notice of it. I have just had a wish for the mountains.

In Amsterdam we knew many people and not a single one has slipped from memory. Just now, dreaming, I am drawn back to a woman painter named Simone and to her fervent romancer, the eternal husband, Dr. Z.

Dr. Z. had the moderate, well-nourished egotism suitable to his small, learned group of colleagues and friends and proper to the educated professional world of Amsterdam. He had his success, some of it medical as a specialist in blood diseases, and some of it amorous. Because of the time he devoted to women he might be surprised to find himself remembered as a *husband*.

In Holland the coziness of life is so complete it cannot even be disturbed by the violent emotional ruptures that tear couples and friends forever apart in other places. Instead, there, first husbands and first wives are always at the same dinner parties and birthday celebrations with their second husbands and wives. Divorces and fractured loves mingled together as if the past were a sort of vinegar blending with the oil of the present. Where could one flee to? New alliances among this restless people were like the rearrangement of familiar furniture. Houses and lives are thus transformed—up to a point. My dear, look, there is a man who plays the violin in the street and there is his son with the saxophone. Coins are falling from the windows. The shadow has passed and everything is in order once more.

She moves into his place. The Herengracht, a great improvement. His wife settles someplace else, taking along her volumes of the existentialist philosophers. What a pleasure to be recombining and yet not going anyplace. The old map of the central city with its faded tintings catches the sunlight.

Dr. Z., all day in his white coat and in the evenings wearing a tie of bright red-and-blue stripes, was born in

Amsterdam. Still the blood of the East runs in his veins. There is something sheikish about him and although there are more flamboyant men around, more handsome and younger, he occupies his space with a kindly, intense assurance. His personal life is rich in variety and yet thoughtful. His originality was that he did not shift so much as acquire.

Fidelity, consideration, sweet-natured uxoriousness were the marks of this faithless husband. In a way, he was like a cripple who yearly enters the hundred-yard dash. Bravo, everyone cried out when he scored. Of course his exploits were not large in number and he was a busy, serious man who was often called to the platform of universities and academies to receive honors. Still, he had his entanglements, rather plain and serious like himself, but worthy, intense, absorbing. Without ever leaving his only wife, he turned each of the women in his life into a wife. Have you paid your taxes? he would say; have you called your mother this week? Oh, dearest, I do not like the sound of that cough.

Many times he was seized by the impulse of flight and thought himself ready or forced by love to "make a new life." But this was impossible for one who could not throw anything away. What a commitment intimacy always is, he would sigh. The sacred flow between men and women, in bed, conversing in a café, talking on the telephone, passing time. What didn't he know about the treacherous, beautiful, golden yoke of time?

Does one still enjoy his old schoolmates, his first cousins? That is not the point. They are your schoolmates, your cousins, and there is always something there, like the enduring presence of your big toe.

* * *

Mevrouw Z.—she had been there forever. They had been separated by the war, but managed to get back together in their same old house. Mevrouw Z. liked to be called Madame Z. because she was French. Small, she must have become in her first youth one of those petite, compact persons who never change, who find a certain exterior style and accept it, as one accepts a piece of architecture for purchase. When her young black hair began to turn gray, she dyed it back to the old color and wore it in the short bob of her youth. The moment she got out of bed in the morning she recolored her eyelashes with black mascara. She wore velvet berets and held firmly to her *look*, which announced like a trumpet that she was not Dutch, she was French. Otherwise she did not conform to any of the notions of a Frenchwoman. She did not cook well, she was not interested in attracting men, she did not have a shrewd hand with household accounts. She let an old Dutchwoman from the country look after the house. Madame Z. was idle except for the enormous amount of reading she did and except for her passion for the French theater. She read about the theater in French papers every day and went to Paris often, taking in a performance every night.

After you had seen her a few times, you found that she was vain but not argumentative. Little appeared to her as new in life, little came as a surprise. It was appealing. She had the idea that a gross, uncomplicated self-interest was the old truth a new force or person were trying to disguise.

Dr. Z., who found the events of his own life flushed with the glow of the unique, the unexpected, the inexplicable, sometimes chewed his lip in annoyance when she expressed her belief in the principle of repetition. They lived in a special intimacy nevertheless.

From Holland I wrote many complaining letters. Dear M.: How cold the house is. How we fight after too much gin, etc., etc.

Complaining letters—and this one of the happiest periods of my life. With what gratitude I look back on Europe for the first time. So, that wraps up Verona. We take in the cracked windows and the brilliant dishevelment of Istanbul. And the long time in Holland, time to take trains, one to Haarlem to see the old almshouse governors painted in their unforgiving black-and-white misery by Frans Hals in his last days. The laughing cavaliers perhaps had eaten too many oysters, drunk too much beer and died a replete, unwilling death, leaving the poor, freed by a bitter life from the killing pleasures, to shrivel on charity, live on with their strong, blackening faces.

Antwerp and Ghent: what wonderful names, he said, hard as the heavy cobbles in the square. Amsterdam, a city of readers. All night long you seemed to hear the turning of pages, pages of French, Italian, English, and the despised German. Those fair heads remembered Ovid, Yeats, Baudelaire and remembered suffering, hiding, freezing. The weight of books and wars.

What are you doing here?
Motley's *Rise of the Dutch Republic* and Fromentin on the old Dutch painters in a neat Phaidon edition.

* * *

Dr. Z. had acquired the nurse in his office. A fresh-looking woman who had never married and who lived frugally outside the center—a long trip on her bicycle. She had her occasional afternoons with Dr. Z., afternoons now grown, according to gossip, as perfunctory and health-giving as a checkup. Oh, the burdens.

Dr. Z. acquired Simone, the painter, after her husband left her. He nudged the other two to make room. Simone was often spoken of as the most independent woman in Amsterdam. She was also the only female painter anyone talked about and it was from her long, nervous struggle to establish herself that the independence had arrived. If indeed it had. She did not display any special happiness or confidence from "doing something well."

Why should painting pictures make you happy? she said. It is not a diversion. Her nerves were frazzled and she had a strong leaning toward melancholy and exhaustion. Yet, worn down by life as she saw herself to be, she was always in movement, always running up and down the stairs to her studio on the fifth floor. In her agitated fatigue, Simone was a striking figure in tattered, mysterious clothes which she apparently bought in junk shops on her travels. Skirts and blouses and jackets of satin or flowered cloth, Balkan decorations, old beads, capes, shawls, earrings. The effect was sometimes that of a deranged frugality and other times she brought it off, like the church dignitaries in Florence when they went in their worn velvets and shredded furs to release the dove from the altar of the Duomo.

Perhaps if she had been a man she would have become a cardinal. She had been born a Catholic and although this had been set aside in the libertarian Amsterdam intellectual world, which was a sort of archive of Trotskyite,

Socialist, Anarchist learning, Simone was sometimes seen slipping into church, wearing several large shawls in pitiful disguise. It was whispered that perhaps she was praying for the soul of her brother, who had collaborated with the Nazis.

Simone's husband looked like an Alpine skier and was instead a professor of history. He actually went off on a long skiing holiday in Austria and in about six months a new woman arrived in Amsterdam, an American. I've always wanted an American, the husband said.

Dr. Z. was sympathetic to Simone and outraged by the husband's complacency and more by his ridiculous happiness with the pretty American. The doctor would have managed differently somehow, in some way, man of binding memories that he was. He took to quoting the Russian proverb mentioned in Pushkin's story "The Captain's Daughter":

If you find someone better than me—you'll
   forget me.
If one who is worse—you'll remember.

Worse? How does he know now, and if it turns out that way it will be too late, Madame Z. insisted.

Slowly, or not so slowly, Dr. Z.'s duet became a trio. He and his wife had known Simone for years. Was that not favorable? Wasn't the ex-husband living with his American in the apartment below Simone's?

Dr. Z. was a passive man *by nature*; that is, he was often led to actions and moods quite the contrary. Certainly at the beginning of his affairs, this natural passivity took an extended leave. He began in a frenzy of passionate feeling. He fell in love; he drank too much; he rushed through his work as quickly as possible and got home very late for dinner and sometimes not until midnight. His nest was shaken by the new windstorm and the squawking of birds began. His wife said this was exactly what she had expected and that it did not interest her. Simone hesitated, but there was the infatuated Dr. Z. with theater tickets. There he was holding fast to her arm as they passed her husband and the American girl at the door of the house. Soon, she said, with a disheartened sigh, that she too was in love.

The nurse cried all day, even in front of the patients. When Simone sometimes called the office, the nurse abused and threatened her.

It is very poor medicine to have nurses in such a state, Simone said. Perhaps another position could be found for her.

Dr. Z. was taken aback but quickly resumed his ground. It's all over with her, he insisted, but I cannot turn away someone I have known and worked with for seven years.

Dr. Z. was jealous of Simone, and her silences filled him with terrible alarm. He pushed his love back a few years. Yes, he remembered being overcome with feeling years ago just at the sight of her buying a book in the square, at a New Year's party when she was wearing green velvet shoes.

I don't remember anything of that sort. Right now is soon enough for me, she said.

At times the doctor did not want to go home at night and announced that he was prepared to give his house to his wife or to set her up in France. For weeks some new plan would seem to be working itself out. Yes, I am working it out, he said to everyone. But then the time came when his mood turned crestfallen and sad. He said Madame Z. hated change.

No one likes change, Simone said. Dr. Z. wept. But it has been more than twenty years. Think of that.

His parents—I knew them and all his living relations and seemed to know the dead ones. Marriage. We would often argue over *interpretation*, so fruitful of conjecture is the text of the family.

He said: You remember that my parents dressed for dinner every night. I thought of it as something military, like people on an army post. His closets were filled with regalia, his large collection of summer and winter dinner jackets, his cummerbunds and patent leather shoes with bows. Do you suppose that is why they imagined—

Or *pretended* to imagine, I said.

Imagined that I would one day give all their money to a wandering monk in brown woolens and sandals.

To me, the parents were a knotty pair. They were in marvelous shape, very careful and prudent. And yet very sensual about fine bed linens, silk underwear, soft cushions, and the proper purring of household motors. The father's fine eyesight, healthy teeth, good tennis game did not keep him from an early death. He died just before we went to Holland and we brought his last days along with us. The mother died soon after we returned.

They would not have liked that, the son said later. Their hearts gave out. Alas, the heart is not a metaphor— or not only a metaphor.

So, the hills of home in the flatness of Holland. Think of it, he would say, our parents were born in the last century. The tsar was out chopping wood for exercise.

In Amsterdam there were no celebrated expatriates

living in the hills or set up in flowery villas near the sea. One week, a lot of snow. Where are we? we wondered. In Iowa City? Many times it was as if the trams were all leading back to home. At night, feeling uprooted because so much was familiar, we would tell each other the story of our lives. The downy, musty embrace of the bed set us afloat, not as travelers, but as ones somehow borne backward to the bricks and stuffs of youth.

We had been to the flower market—a thousand still lives. People, rushing about the Leidseplein, revealed ghostly similarities to those we had left behind. Old accusations: that is the memory left by mothers and fathers. Or is it we, in recall, who are accusing? So, in the chill, the litany of exiles, in the old language.

He remembered what a disappointment he had been to his grandfather, how the old man, dying of cancer, would call out to him, the only male around since a handsome son had died at thirty. Who are you? Grandfather would ask. One year thin and handsome and the next year bulky and brooding. Cannot shoot a gun, cannot ride a horse. What prizes have you won, except for collecting snakes and mismatched socks? On a sailboat, a menace. Where are you standing, *why* are you standing gazing at the water? You will drown us all.

The stove died, the snow clung to the panes, the outline of fringed lamps caught the light of the street. In the shadows, listening to the bells ringing the hours, we would lie smoking and talking.

History assaults you and if you live you are restored to the world of gossip. That is what it had been for Dr. Z. He was half-Jewish and had spent time in a labor camp in Germany. This well-established Nederland lover, with his nervous alliances and peculiar fidelities, had looked death in the eye, had lived through the extermination of his younger brother. This life, his aura, remained in his proud, olive-tinted eyes, in his researches on the devastations flowing in the bloodstream, in his death-defyng lovemaking. He was a small, shrewd European country, moving about carefully in peacetime, driven on by the force of ghastly memories.

So, life after death is to fall in love once more, to set up a little business, to learn to drive a car, take airplane trips, go to the sun for vacations.

It began to appear that Simone was not suited to the role of mistress. She said: This thing has brought a great coarsening of my nature. I hate Madame Z. What is she, a general? She seems to be giving a good many orders to those of us behind the lines.

Hate? Dr. Z. said. That's quite extreme. She has her qualities.

When Simone saw the wife on the street she rushed off in the opposite direction. So fearful was she of a meeting she would not go to her friends' houses without making careful inquiries.

The whole of their circle in Amsterdam was involved in the affair. This wish to oust Madame Z. and the nurse is Simone's cardinal side, people decided. Yes, the little girl who held the hand of so many nuns cannot accept the purgatory of Dr. Z.'s confusing nature and intentions.

One time Madame Z. went to Paris for several weeks. With a round-trip ticket of course, Simone observed bitterly. But in the freedom, she and the doctor went for a weekend to London to look at pictures. It was not a happy time. Dr. Z. was always calling Paris to speak to his wife or calling his office to speak to the nurse. Telling them tremendous lies about a "conference." Simone spent most of her time in London saying: It will soon be over and we will be back where we started.

Dearest darling, do not rush to future pain, the doctor said. But all went as she had predicted. Back once more, Simone could be seen several evenings a week at the window of her top floor, looking down on the street, waiting for the hurried approach of her lover. And late in the night when he was returning to his wife, Simone would open the shutters and wave a long goodbye to the swarthy, badly dressed, vivacious man, now turning a corner and fading from sight.

Dr. Z. was happy in his love pains. He adored to spend the evening in Simone's studio, smoking a cigarette, drinking coffee, eating little chocolate cakes and sipping gin. He was honestly more and more in love and the genuineness of his feelings often caused Simone to burst into tears of anger.

Dr. Z. had studied the body and its workings and liked to say: We human beings are, *au fond*, put together quite simply. Yes, quite simply. The part that is complicated, even we as scientists are ignorant of that.

In matters of love he seemed to feel the same. His distressing trio caused him to be often fretful, sleepless, anxious, jealous, even drunken. But he also knew well the dejection of resignation and the torture of absence. So, tormented, accused, even guilty, there was still happiness to be found in reassuring the weeping nurse at the end of the day, in bringing home a *pâté* and cheese to his wife, in going down a dark canal on the arm of Simone and singing "In questa tomba oscura." Somehow he could lend to the noble composition a heartfelt flirtatiousness.

During our year in Holland there was at last a movement of reclamation on the part of Simone. She broke off with the doctor and stayed in the house for weeks for fear of meeting him and once more surrendering to his passion for her. He whistled below the window, potted tulips arrived. Look at the colors! A late Mondrian, no? his note would say.

He called upon the help of European poetry:

Alas for me, where shall I get the flowers when it is winter and where the sunshine and shadow of earth? The walls stand speechless and cold, the weather vanes rattle in the wind.

Simone was assisted by an attack of depression and did not turn back. She hurt the doctor's feelings by saying: I do not seem to care for anyone just now. Least of all myself.

The doctor's wife and the nurse were affronted by Simone's revolt. They accused her of triviality and shallowness, of heartlessness. The doctor's sufferings fell alike upon them, as if it were a contagion. His alarm, his loss, his humiliation were an insult to themselves. And perhaps the two women, so accustomed to his ways, sensed that the singularity of endings may slowly gather into a plural.

* * *

Love affairs with their energy and hope do not arrive again and again, forever. So, you no longer play tennis, no longer move from place to place in the summer, no longer understand what use you can make of the sight of the Andes or the columns of Luxor.

It gradually became clear that Simone would not be replaced. Poor Dr. Z. with his infidelities and agreeable lies, his new acquisitions and engaging disruptions: they vanished suddenly but so quietly and naturally he was the last to know.

Wasn't it said about Queen Elizabeth that old age took her by surprise, like a frost?

In a few years the nurse went home to retire, to look after her old mother in the country. Simone died. It turned out that she had done more than a dozen portraits of Dr. Z. and one sold to an American museum for a fair price. In it, Dr. Z. is seen in a white jacket and there are instruments of his profession about him. On the wall, not one, but three stylized skeletons are dangling from hooks.

1973

The doctor and his wife are in New York for a conference. I go to meet them at a shabby, depressing hotel in the West 70's where Europeans who are not rich often stay.

They were like two woolen dolls and I could not decide whether the Frenchwoman had grown to the size of the Dutchman or whether he had, with a courteous condescension, simply inclined downward to the size of his little French wife. She was still wearing her black beret, and her fingernails shone with a wine-colored polish. She spoke in tongues: Dutch, German, French, and English, as if choosing cakes from a tray.

Dr. Z. met a mild New York winter day clothed in Siberian layers. He was wearing a heavy black overcoat, a woolen vest, a dark-gray sweater, and when he sat down in the waiting room off the lobby gray winter underwear appeared above his socks.

He talked, he told the Amsterdam gossip, he spoke of his work, of the fearful cost of things, of hippies in Vondel Park.

Madame Z. smoked cigarettes and coughed. They were studying the map of the city, looking for subway and bus lines. The outstanding difficulties of thrift in New York bewildered them, and they sat there as if pulled down into the mud of a dismaying displacement, the confusion that afflicts unfashionable, elderly foreigners when they visit America. They who had been everywhere, from Jakarta to Tokyo to India and every country in Europe.

Dr. Z. smiled and bowed and dashed about looking for chairs and a quiet corner. In fact he seemed to be groping in the New York air for the supports of his life in Amsterdam, for his weathered little house on the Amstel, with his office on the first floor, and the rooms above with the old patterned carpets, the comfort of the hideous abstractions given by patients, abstractions which covered the walls next to the stairs like so many colored water spots left over from an old leak.

Where is my life? he seemed to be saying. My plates of pickled mussels, the slices of cheese, the tumblers of lemon gin?

Still, importance flickered in his eyes—his olive eyes

still shining with the oil of remembered vanity and threatening to water with the tears of all he had learned and forgotten in his long life.

We in Holland were the first to do certain important blood studies, he said. I no longer have my laboratory at the hospital but I keep up with the developments in my field. How can one not? A life's work.

We in Holland kept appearing in his conversation. The vastness of the skies they had flown over and the large abyss into which they had fallen on the ground made him call forth his country like an ambassador, one who stands for the whole.

You remember that he was well known there, his wife said without any special inflection. Oh, I know, I know. I remember well the well-known Dr. Z.

Enough of that, he said. Edam cheese is better known than any Dutchman. That it is well to recall, also.

As it got to be near six o'clock I asked if they wanted to go to a nearby Irish saloon for a drink. The doctor drew back with a frightened look, but his wife took up the suggestion vehemently. Indeed yes she would like a drink she said with a peculiar insistence and defiance.

We sat in a dark booth and Madame Z. ordered a martini. An American martini, she said twice. The doctor crumpled and sagged over a beer, a Heineken.

Supporting home industries, his wife said.

Suddenly in the gloom, Madame Z. began her lilting harangue, all of it pouring forth with a fearful energy. She did not use to talk very much, the doctor said, attempting a smile. See the unbeckoned, unpredicted changes of age, the sky full of falling stars!

It was clear that the recitation was not new and that in the midst of it she could pause only to order another drink.

I have always hated Holland. I am not Dutch. I am French, born in Paris.

There are many Frenchmen, the doctor interrupted. It is not what I would call a special distinction in itself.

She went on. There are many Dutchmen too and all alike. The men and the women. The provincialism. Can you imagine a country proud of skinny Indonesians, dark and slow and surly primitives, serving in red coats? *Rijstaffel*—a joke. Nuts and raisins and bananas. I would rather have herring, if the choice must be made . . . And it must be made or starve . . . But the worst thing is the ugliness of the people. Who can tell the men and the women apart in their rotten mackintoshes, their rubber-soled shoes . . . Look at the Queen—a joke. And old Wilhelmina in her tweeds like a buffalo . . . And the weather, steaming like hell in the summer and drizzling sleet the rest of the year. *Drizzling*, is that English? . . . What is going on in Amsterdam, tell me? Someone playing the organ in a church. They think they are masters of culture when they speak French, but if you want to write something you write it in Dutch, which no one reads. And why should they? Even the Poles are better off. Warsaw is a real city, not a puppet-show setting like Amsterdam.

Her black, black hair, her tiny little black feet, her wine-colored fingers heavy with red and green semiprecious stones set in gold. She was like an old glazed vessel, veined and cracked, but nevertheless in one piece.

The doctor trembled. This is not what you would call a discussion, he said.

And turning aside he made an effort to change the

awful flow. I am not a patriot, he said, still couldn't I claim that the Dutch are a civilized people? A bit tiresome about the loss of Indonesia and all that, perhaps, but . . .

Indonesia! she shrieked and the bartender shrugged. How all of you used to complain when you had to go out there to lecture, to advise as you called it. To visit the rich men on their plantations. Little cries all night about the bugs and the humidity. The suffering sweat of the lordly Dutchman. Imagine Holland with colonies. Have you ever seen the so-called city of Paramaribo? It's a scandal, a joke.

Madame Z. tottered to her feet, exhausted. The doctor took her arm and gave a sigh as deep as death itself. Out on the street in the cold wind he supported his tiny little wife who could not stand alone. She dangled on his arm like a black shopping bag. For the moment she was quiet and he attempted a lighthearted manner, a whispered addition.

As you can see, she has taken to drink in a disastrous fashion. A sigh and then he bowed with something of his old sheikishness, drawing me into his memories.

It's all those love affairs, especially the darling Simone. They don't forgive you after all. They have their revenge.

It seemed to soothe the doctor to try to take the blame, as if even the revenge brought him back to his younger days. It was not clear whether he believed what he was saying. The ruefulness of his smile.

As we neared the hotel he said bitterly, It is only eight o'clock. But what can we do except go to bed without dinner? She will sleep it off and not remember a thing, the way they do. So mysterious. Yes, she must go to bed.

Bed! Madame Z. cried out, calling upon her last breath. They are all terrible lovers. Frauds, everyone of them. Fiascoes!

They passed into the brown and gray lobby, old companions sad but not quite miserable. They are waving goodbye. He is bowing and she is now winking and smiling.

She has hit the doctor like the Spanish Fury, but fortunately he is accustomed to the wind from the North Sea. Her hat askew and a strand of hair slanted down her cheek, Madame Z. of Paris had at last become Dutch, needing only a few strewn oyster shells and a ragged dog to bring to mind those tippling, pipe-smoking women in the paintings of the seventeenth century, creatures of the common life the Dutch bourgeoisie were pleased to commission and purchase.

Part Nine

SOME HAVE been here in this house in New York, have been here mopping, cleaning greasy stoves, putting in their hours, their weeks. One was in another city, in Boston; one up in Maine, living through winter after winter, a decade falling like snow on the top of another, soundless.

When I think of cleaning women with unfair diseases I think of you, Josette. When I must iron or use a heavy pot for cooking, I think of you, Ida. When I think of deafness, heart disease and languages I cannot speak, I think of you, Angela. Great washtubs full of sheets remind me of more than one.

I came up here to Maine in service long ago, Ida said. I came as a girl, with the family, to the summer house. They kept saying how beautiful Maine was and one summer I just stayed . . . Words of a rough and peculiar laundress.

The passion for the seamless collar under the iron, for the grating of the vacuum cleaner, the shine of wax on the floor, water forced out of dirty mops, beds tight as a bandage. The energy of the lustful movements, whiteness of towels, scoured garbage pails. Ferocious battles with repetition, with the sloth of others, the crumbs and dust, the gathering of ashes, the adhesion of eggs, burnt pans and blackened ovens. At some point in the day, finally things in place, for a moment.

Intolerable beatitude in the rhythm of slaves and behind the passions: necessity, disguise, habit, will.

I am thinking of Josette and Ida, remembering them here in my study in New York where the moths will soon arrive, the lipstick stain on the white door will never be washed away, the lost garnet pin will not turn up, nor will the windows ever be free of exhaust streaks from old trucks, and the faucet will never cease to drip its grassy-green trail.

Heroines, turning their key in the lock of the door in the morning, arriving like a wanted medicine or even some entrance of perfect happiness. Josette, in Boston, long ago. The blessing of her white nylon uniform, her heavy rubber-soled shoes, the benign flash of gray false teeth, the crown of stiff gray hair cut in a plain bob, the grayish-brown skin cool as steel. Beauty formed out of negatives. She raced up and down the steep stairs of Marlborough Street, and the stairs of other old town houses, malignant ascensions and descensions of space and privilege, punishing the legs, the heart and the disposition for the glory of dining rooms with twelve chairs spaced around the wall, for the large rectangles of parlors, one at the front, one at the back.

* * *

Rilke imagined that a tin lid had no other desire than to rest evenly and firmly upon its proper can. The old lights of Rand Avenue in summer, the playground, the band concerts, lids and cans trying to fit. And if they fit, or seem to do so, early in life, most of those older shudder a bit.

Josette, childless, had a husband she had met in high school—Michael. Their toil began, no doubt from the moment they met and saw their lives streaming out from the meeting. First love—all is given for eternity, and these two, loyal and fearful, had about them a mystery, the mystery of orphans. Michael was painfully uncertain and yet trusting. Together they shared a humbleness and courtesy made up of poverty and thrift, of neatness and diffidence. Both grew up in Lawrence, Massachusetts; both were from French-Canadian families who had come down to work in the factories.

Boston: an intermission. Many things happen between the acts. Everything has come to me and been taken from me because of moving from place to place. Anyway, it was some time there in the beautiful city, the city filled with names.

Connais-tu le pays? Yes, everyone knows Boston, even I. How is the Mister this morning? Josette would say. The Mister? Shall I turn his devastated brown hair to red, which few have? Appalling disarray of trouser and jacket and feet stuffed into stretched socks. Kindly smile, showing short teeth like his mother's.

* * *

Dearest M.: You ask me about his life in Boston. It is odd that, since this is his city, we do not seem quite to belong here. Of course I am like an Eskimo sent to a circus, dressed in whale grease. But he? Thirty-six is neither young enough nor old enough for certain places, but perhaps in the end this city will interest him as it did when he was young. Now, a lot of people seem to think he's an anarchist (they strive to be a little out-of-date) and he does often have the preoccupied look of a secret agent. Just as always he reads and writes all day, here in this house on the top floor, drinks quarts of milk, smokes cigarettes. He hates for me to play my jazz records, but sometimes I do late at night and then he dances around, off the beat, like a bear.

His health? All right. There is an absurd little midget of a doctor here, a psychiatrist, sweet as a chaplain, very conventional and timid, accustomed to treating and advising wellborn Boston women who have stayed too long at home and young men not doing very well at the State Street Trust. He does not in this case seem to know the difference.

What distresses the doctor, makes him look at his watch, are long "free associations" about Goethe. Is he a family connection? the little doctor asked. Well, that's not a scandal, I guess, since the man got out of school almost a century after the Brahmin Germanism.

How long ago was it, Josette? Twenty years. I will remember a type, not unexpected. An old lady, tall and thin, looking exactly as she should, being an old Boston lady who is a *character*.

Age and her very long legs had given her the horse

aspect. She, true to image, gave tiresome tea parties on a Sunday afternoon and invited to them dull students from client states, from Taiwan and Korea. The students' yellow faces and stiff hair slipped into the gloom of her dusty mansion near the Athenaeum. The old lady knew a little, but not much, as it would be because she had always had money and no profession and so her mind swoops and darts and flys away.

Queer, impudent decline, a *sight*, free, open on Sunday, galloping about the tall parlors on her long horse legs. Braying assurance of tone. She would say: What a pity, no more Socialist party. And: Henry Adams was the ugliest man I ever laid eyes on.

She had a curious wish to catch the learned in a byway of ignorance. Because she was a Boston spectacle, a number of gifted persons had come along during her lifetime—had come into the depressing parlors where she sat behind a tray of tarnished silver and offered English muffins which had been toasted in the morning and were as hard as cement. Sometime during the party, she would point to several old prints on the wall and announce with a sly grin:

I showed those little things to Panofsky once and he was stumped. Absolutely stumped. But, Professor, I said, they are simple *vues optiques*. That is all, ordinary *vues optiques*.

The old lady, lively as she was, had in a positive, outstanding way the deepest incuriosity. Biographies of maids, bodies of guests, were observed by her only by accident, the way things suddenly glare forth on a platter, quickly, in a blur. No doubt the incuriosity was the source of her attachment to anecdote, to the set piece of conversation with its tag line.

Yet, her last year of life was a marvel. In her eighty-seventh year she found an adorable friend. A chattering, high-spirited bird of a young man came into the gloom of the old house, which had not been painted for years. That is, he came as a visitor, a new friend, almost violently happy to be with her among the old portraits and valuables, the broken Chippendale, the dangerous, loosely caned chairs, the recent pie-tins from frozen-food counters. He was what was then in antique circles called a "fairy" —and he flew in to her from the clutter of Somerville, the compost heap behind the Harvard Yard.

The young man adored the old lady and most gratifying of all was that he believed her to be a *character*; he saw her precisely as she herself did, without reservation. Yes, she was indeed an old Boston pedigreed specimen and this was astonishingly agreeable to both of them, this being her own image. He raced in and out of the house, not waiting for invitations; he ran up and kissed the muddled white head; he made the servant laugh with his Irish brogue imitations. He loved to look at her family photographs and when he saw her sitting on a rock near the ocean, wearing long black swimming drawers, he would say, *fantastic*. Or here she was more than half a century ago at a lawn party. You look fabulous, he cried out. The hat, the hat, marvelous!

It was genuine because he himself was a character also, a living, sturdy weed of gossip and laughter, of racing confessions about nights of fun and errors, of cooking recipes with unexpected olives, of fish sprinkled with chocolate.

She was nearing senility and he was a wound-up toy. They had a good time together and, in the end, inspired with honor and love, she left him a good deal of her money. She paid her bill.

Dear Folks: Do not be too proud of me. Be careful of that.
    Love to everyone,
    Elizabeth

Josette raced around Boston like a migrant bird. Sometimes Irish maids, fresh-faced even into old age from birth in a countryside somewhere, were taken aback by her industrial grayness, that discoloring gene of the mills and the shoe factory. Josette came by the day, one house on Monday and another on Wednesday; the Irish maids cooked cod-cakes in the morning and soup and roasts at night and lived in small rooms hidden in great houses.

Grave disasters behind Josette's swiftness. Beatings in childhood.

Once over a cup of coffee she told of having been raped by someone in the family and would not say who it was. It seemed to connect in my mind with the loss of her teeth, which, of course, came later. The cold of Canada, wet fur. No, it was not the most important thing in her life, she insisted—and long, long ago. But you remembered it? Remembered, well, that yes, she answered.

Josette's mind was much occupied by a monstrous sister, still living in Lawrence. It was not affection so much as confusion of feeling that held her. And in a way she was thrilled by the power of her sister's aberrations. We drove to Lawrence so that I might see for myself the outrageous, interesting invalidism in which the sister, coarse and homely as an old boot, lived, or reigned.

She was unparalleled indeed; one of those possessive, demanding persons who can demand and receive, can throttle and enclose others in a way undreamed of by the reasonable. The sister was transfixed by the spectacle of her incapacities, lifted up to peaks of feeling by every ache and pain, quick to throw the magic of her sufferings into the air like crooked smiles. Buried intelligence gave a dimension to her rigidity, brought to it the structure of an intense bookkeeping, without an error, directed upon herself.

The sister sat in her wheelchair, the queenly owner of her arthritis—very much the way that stockings are advertised in *queen* sizes for those weighing from 270 to 350 pounds.

She sat, enormous and riveting, as she wheeled about the little apartment, the upstairs of one side of an old rotting clapboard two-family house. Doctors, years ago, had insisted she was not paralyzed. They screwed up their faces in annoyance at her perverse and determined defiance. No matter, she refused exercises for the joints, refused operations, refused to *try*, turning away every suggestion of amelioration as if threatened by a rival. She grew large and helpless, fat and weak, crippled and combative.

It was known that sometimes the sister howled all night in her pride in the pain of her affliction. The cries and complaints gained substance in the minuteness of description, the persecutions deeply pondered.

* * *

Josette, by the time I met her, had already had both of her breasts hacked off by cancer, and other complications drifted about her in a whisper. She approached the mutilation from a distance, the place reserved for graying hair and wrinkles at the edge of the eyelids, something slow and common, *there*.

(Diseases. When I would fly home during the year, coming down at the Bluegrass airport, it seemed to me that sweet and cheerful greetings were always mixed with the warm handshake of diabetes, hernias, high blood pressure, cataracts, hysterectomies, prostate troubles.)

The sister circled about Josette's lost breasts and her thinness and having taken them in still placed it all under a benevolent dispensation.

See Josette run about, she would say. For myself I am lucky to be able to crawl to the door and throw myself down the stairs when the time comes . . .

The halo of invalidism rose over her brow.

Ministering angels: she, quarrelsome, petty, deformed and stubborn, had a few years back taken in a young man as a boarder. These things happen. People without the room to breathe in take in lodgers and ill-fed people put up signs advertising breakfast.

Soon the boarder was a companion, an accomplice caught up in her wild frozen life as intensely as herself. He came, fair-faced and inward, with the groceries after his day at the plant. He pushed the chair to the porch and usually got his huge charge into the car for a Sunday drive—in and out, carefully lifting and arranging, with a passionate, peculiar attentiveness, representing a defiant victory.

He talked and he listened. They shared suspicion of human intentions, and their eyes glittered over the downcasting news from the shop, the delinquency of neighbors, the bad character of the neglectful and ungrateful.

Throughout our visit, Josette smiled, sighed, and trembled as the victim wheeled to the cookie plate, approached the coffee on the stove, spun around in pursuit of spoon, sugar. Toward the end, Josette crumpled under the spell, grew grave and meek. Later she remarked that her sister was growing fatter and fatter and shriveling at the same time.

One night, a few months later, the sister fell into violent illness. The young man, fearing her demand not to be moved, feared death more. He called an ambulance amidst her groans and accusations, and the heavy, heavy figure was carried off to the hospital, to lie there in the waiting room among the injured and screaming who knew nothing of illness, who contemptibly let life and death near them with no sense at all of possibilities, lengthy martyrdoms.

Not a one of them, she whimpered, knew of years in wheelchairs, of the improvisations, accommodations and interior assets she had piled up.

The sister had many diseases at the end. She listened carefully, her eyes wide, to the listing of them all: diabetes, kidney disease, heart disease and also arthritis.

* * *

She died. The young man closed the door on himself, scarcely going out except to the shop from which he returned with the groceries, now a bag of prepared foods. She was the only mother I ever had, he said. Josette came back from the Mass and the burial deeply ashamed, but not able to figure out the exact shape of any of it.

A brilliant night outside in New York City. It is Saturday and people with debts are going to restaurants, jumping in taxicabs, careening from West to East by way of the underpass through the Park. What difference does it make to be here alone? Even now, just after eight in the evening, the trucks are starting their delivery of the Sunday *Times*.

After a year, more than a year, I return to you, Josette. In the meantime I have been to Honolulu and to Russia. A lifetime of worrying and reading may bring you at last to free trips you are not sure you wish to take. In the company of others not sure they should spare the time just now. You, so poor and hard pressed, would be interested to know that there are many cleaning women standing about in the halls of the hotels of Russia. Curious— they do not often enter the rooms. The remains of the first day's sturgeon stayed all week on the plate, on the table next to the bed.

Josette had a love story, suitable to her old-fashioned struggle and to the steady, slow, determined pace of little expectation that must nevertheless be achieved. Michael was a small, insecure man, not very bright and always nervously working. The automobile shop filled him with anxiety and love, the anxiety of love perhaps. The men in the shop came into his conversation in whispers. Some of them he adored for their brightness, toughness and worldliness; some with bad tempers, indolence and carelessness haunted him. Ill-educated, with fear of displeasing, Michael was like a man of an earlier century, hierarchical, with himself at the bottom.

He dreamed of cars and finally one of his dreams came true when he bought a secondhand Buick. Its virtues, its mileage, its fine engine, its low price (close to stealing to get such a fine car for that, he said again and again): and himself at the wheel, ears tuned to every crunch and whine. He was happy, except for the horror of dents administered by others.

Sometimes on Sunday morning he would drive up the alley of Marlborough Street and gaze upon our own car. There he was in a brown hat, meditating. He caressed the car with a soft cloth, lifted the front and stared long at the inside. Inspection of battery, contemplation of tires.

Josette all day long dusted vases from France, swept over Oriental rugs, admired marble mantles and brought elaborate brass andirons to a high shine. She made up beds with antique spreads, looked into mirrors with eagles on them—and on the weekends and vacations she and Michael got into the Buick and drove off to trailer parks.

Many, many beautiful memories they had of the way the water and lights hooked up, the wandering people with their news of other parks, good sites and bad, the comradeship, the radio, the cans of beans for the miraculous little stove, the cans of beer from the perfect cooler.

Josette, in her passionate neatness, adored small places, metals that shone in blues and pinks and pale greens. She loved packaged mashed potatoes and frozen patties. And then there was always the car, the object for which they worked and saved. The trailer park, itself, was the hymn sung to the automobile, saying that a car was indeed their true home. The mobile home, the large box, resting on its plot, asleep, dreaming of the road, dreaming of being pulled along forever, someplace beyond.

Michael, of course, was struck with a terrible illness that mangled his life. It is possible to say *of course* because there had never been any certain promises in his life and his lack of brightness of mind, along with his dutifulness, caused him to be fearful. He was one of those men who acted as if he expected to be shouted out and would not know how to reply.

A blood clot in his leg threatened his life and changed his life in a moment. He was never again well and yet he rose up out of bed, weak and crippled, thinking madly of the job, the job. He stumbled back to the car shop, desperately punishing himself, miserable and yet, blinking anxiously behind his yellowish spectacles, he would mumble about "return in six months" and never called the doctor to inquire about the appropriateness of symptoms during the interval.

He and so many deprived others I have known seemed afraid of bothering doctors, of acting out of turn, of complaining, and so they went on, the far-off appointment in their mind as if waiting for a reward or a lottery drawing.

* * *

At the shop, his face in a grimace that tried to be a grin of health, his condition worsened and he was forced to quit. For several weeks he was like a madman, and Josette was as gray as death, gray enough for her own and his.

Then a stroke of blessing, wonder. Michael got a job as janitor for a nice building in the Back Bay, working mostly for the accommodation of the basement apartment they were given.

He loved it and all of a sudden he was loved. Loved by the tenants, by the owners, for his neatness, his willingness, his devotion to the building itself. It filled his heart with passionate attachment, stepped in the sore place that had been left empty and aching by his departure from the car shop.

In the evenings, Michael painted all the basement walls. He set out scrubbed, beautiful garbage cans in rows. He stacked his tools and hoses, hung implements on nails, carried suitcases to lockers and would empty a whole bin in order to arrange stored things to size.

The little apartment with its half kitchen and small icebox shone and became the pure, neat square they both loved. Sitting at the card table for supper they were like nothing so much as strange, worn, contented dolls, placed on a shelf.

Their pleasure in the place expanded, and the poor cripple lifted more and more, worked harder and harder. At last with the backward, perverse turn of fate, like that of a bitter fairy tale, his gasping, obsessive toil appalled the owners of the house, created in the minds of contented tenants an accompanying sense of foreboding and guilt, an idea that it was death itself hosing down the sidewalk, polishing the door knocker. They persuaded him to quit.

Josette and Michael gave up and took on their destiny. They "retired" on a pittance to Florida, where the sun came down on the trailer parks. The Buick was retired, too, seeming to metamorphose into a mobile home.

A year later I received a card from Josette:

I lost Michael. He died instantly at the checkout counter of a supermarket, where he was working.

I see pink lights in their trailer and Josette and Michael are there watching television, side by side with others in identical pastel oblongs. It is institutional and comforting, what they like, similar to an old orphanage, a busy circumscribed space where equals gather.

Perhaps it seems to them that the rest of their life was lived in a dubious foster home, one of those dead improving transactions—sly, calculating, private accommodations in a tomb of strangers. Their trailer park—at last they have reached it, earned it.

Their trailer, like the others, is neat, but the opposite of a spartan fitness. Instead they are living in a disguise created out of fantasy. Every object is in the shape of something foreign to it. A clock is a ship's wheel, the blue aluminum of the outside leads into a brown darkness of walls stained to look like the paneled cellars of castles. Early American rag rugs made of nylon, white picket fences, rocking chairs of knotty pine, many things that oddly wish to say, Grandmother.

The rain on the flat tin—that must be nice, as it turns the warm dust to mud.

* * *

Josette—the gap of Marlborough Street and Beacon Hill. All her grayness was filled with light and it is an embarrassment to speak of one so good. In a wine-colored pillbox hat perched on her harsh hair, she came for a visit once to New York, while they were still in the reassurance of the apartment house basement. But everything is here, she said. The true highboy and the false sideboard.

I am sure she too has died. To him was given heart disease and to her, cancer. They are both gone, with all their questions unanswered.

After the death of their loved servant, Rose, the Goncourts spoke of her twenty-five years of care, of shared joys and sorrows, of her devotion, "the sort one hopes will be present to shut one's eyes for the last time."

On the day of Rose's death—"the irony of things"— they were asked for the first time to dine with Princess Mathilde. A few days later they learned of the real life of Rose, of her "nocturnal orgies," her secret childbearings, her debts, her jealous, ugly passion for the son of the dairywoman, a passion that killed her when she stood out all night in the rain spying on him. From these revelations the Goncourts learned what? To be forever "suspicious of all womankind," and to be forever mindful of a woman's "genius for lying."

Another summer, now 1972. A circle of fog around Ida's cottage. A window is open and so she is still there. And since she is alive she is doing people's laundry—one fact assumes the next.

* * *

Maine. Caribou and Moosehead, awesome, rare creatures. In midsummer, ruthless, weedy wildflowers, berries hanging from the boughs of mountain ash, starlings in the alders, the spidery brambles of old blackberry bushes. A rush of heat enters the town like the roar of motorcycles on Sunday. Sunset nevertheless will bring a cool wind that rattles the windows. The islands are filled with well-to-do frosty American specimens, summering. Someone water-skis on the bay and the sight is almost indecorous. If the heat continues then the wilderness will be threatened with drought and fire. It is not possible to have a true summer without excess up here in the north; the excess that is summer threatens the natural damp, windy woods which, even if you have never seen them are always present in your mind.

Inside the door of Ida's house, her large black winter galoshes are standing, a premonition in August of the Maine winter. She knows where she is. In the same way a child's sled has been propped up all summer against the front door of a house in town. At Ida's, beet greens are on the stove and she is corning beef. The steady rhythm of her day, her season. For her breakfast, thick slices of bacon; a big black pan in which eggs float like water lillies. While they fry she will examine the sky of the day.

Large head, large teeth, large carpet slippers and the large arms that have been wringing, pulling, lifting for a lifetime. All of the large parts of the body hurt in some way, even if all are strong.

1950
This evening I met Ida for the first time. Twice a week she goes touring about town, driven by the owner of the

hardware store, and she makes her laundry deliveries. Groans and loud, hoarse laughter as she hauls first herself and then the laundry baskets out of the sinking back seat. Not much over thirty years old then, but no hint of youth except for the curls which have been formed by pins clamped next to her ears. Reddish curls, large, round, reddish face, and a voice large and reddish.

The wicker basket is heavy with linen sheets and pillow-cases, with white towels. On the top are folded the blouses, silk nightgowns and petticoats she refers to as "body clothes." Her money is counted out and on she goes to the next house on the square, and then down to the large summer houses overlooking the bay. Finicky patrons mutter about scorchings, but softly, because she is known to be tough and to flare into anger, coming at you with a pugilistic glare in her light, pink eyes.

The spring was awful wet, she screams. Potatoes are nothing but water.

Her lyrical utterance is saved for her work. She admits that she loves wash out on the line. That's where it is lovely and fresh, she insists, her voice rising.

Ida's bungalow stands up on a hill near a tidal river. It is hers, she paid for it, built it, and over the years scarcely ever leaves it. No family and, like country people, no scenery for friendship; neighbors, yes, who drive her to Bucksport to the market once in a while. She gets huge loaves of white bread and a few things from a grocery truck that comes by once a week and then there is canning going on in her kitchen all summer—canning for the long winter. She is too heavy and stubborn for movement, too difficult and independent for anything except work.

* * *

1960's—perhaps it was her bungalow standing there in the quiet, visible if not beckoning. Neat and sturdy on its cement foundation.

The wind rustled the trees, the mailbox rusted, the coldest of stars seemed right on top of the little house at night. But inside there was this fat, strong, woman and the shining black stove heating up day and night, and the wide old feather bed with its oaken headpost and its quilts and comforters.

Disaster came in the early sixties. Ida began to be visited by Herman, a local man, one of the native families. Herman appeared and disappeared, off and on, setting himself up in a shack next to his old father. Sometimes he arrived for a year and went away for as long; sometimes he stayed a few months only. He mumbled about working somewhere on ships, since he had grown up on the sea; he talked of a bit of clam-digging or of shrimping in the South.

He was dark, thin and tall, with a disagreeable, cranky hermit inwardness, broken now and then by disconcerting jerks of rapid reminiscence. In these remembering talks, his long yellow teeth emerged like fog lights out of the taciturn lips, his wandering eyes glistened with the recall of drinking bouts, of crewing on yachts in the Caribbean.

About these claims Ida would later say with a sneer: I'd as soon have a baboon without thumbs on board as him.

His periods of torpor had their content, however; sullen schemes, petty maneuvers, small thefts, borrowing, dumb plans for curious businesses.

Herman is most horrible to behold sitting in the back seat of the delivery car on a Friday afternoon, huddled among the laundry baskets, glowering with chagrin or sometimes taking on a sort of official air, as if he were Ida's manager.

For a time he is safe in the big feather bed. But there was the problem of the day, while the tubs boiled, the wringer squeaked, the iron filled the house with its steamy smells. They got up at daylight and sometimes at seven he walked "down street" and spent the morning talking to the men on the wharf, the boatbuilders in their crowded shed. At noon he would walk home to eat boiled cabbage and potatoes, stews and the beer he had bought with money taken from the tin candy box, hidden behind the stove.

Slowly the sound of the old Maytag churning began to have an unsettling effect upon Herman and he could be heard groaning curses at it. She screamed back in their violent defense and assault. Ida liked fighting and arguing and was known to be a dangerous enemy. Naturally she hated everything Herman was—shifty, idle, a wandering isolate, with a morose and needy nature that could when the need was upon him attach itself somewhere.

The winter came down upon them. The suicide season arrived early. The land, after a snowfall, would turn into a lunar stillness, satanic, brilliant. The tall trees, altered by the snow and ice, loomed up in the arctic landscape like ancient cataclysmic formations of malicious splendor. The little houses on the road with their stoves and furnaces blowing heat, their lamps glowing, trembling there in the whiteness, might be settlements waiting for a doom that would come over them silently in the night.

The nightmare closeness in the cottage, frozen, combative wills. What could that man talk about in the winter? There was nothing he knew, she said.

Out of bed and into the kitchen, she greeting the glacial dawn the same as ever. He—dark, sallow, morbid. They were both going mad and the heat of the stove where the iron warmed and the food boiled was the heat of hell.

In a time of thaw, Herman's moroseness thawed to a glittering, nervous malice. By this time, Ida had learned that he had the soul and body of a convict. He had been in and out of jail, sometimes going in to flee the cold or simply to be someplace. In the same way he had come to her—a jail sentence.

But the parole spirit was on him and dull schemes began to enter his mind once more. He began to mutter that the house was half his own and the very words led her to scream and fight so fiercely the police were called. Among the neighbors there was a question of which one would be killed first.

One day, Herman vanished for good. He took with him everything of use he could find in the house—her little store of money, a war bond, her savings account book, which he threw in the gutter, a worthless brooch. These things grew in Ida's mind to such a heat and rage that she was taken to the insane asylum for a few months.

She raged and clawed and threatened her way out and came back to her house, her baskets of clothes, her pots of boiled beef and turnips, the companionate ironing board and mopping pail.

The present summer now. One too many with the gulls, the cry of small boats on the strain, the soiled sea, the sick clam. A few hours ago I made the journey to Ida's house, knocked on the latched screen door and felt something close to fright coming over me. Oh, God, there she is, homely, homely, scabby with a terrible skin rash, heavy in her cotton housedress, lame in her carpet slippers, pushing to the door with painful, heavy slowness. She is violently cheerful. The baskets of laundry waiting to be picked up are now of red-and-blue latticed plastic.

Her large, muscled arms hold me for a moment in a pounding embrace. The smell of laundry is, truly, like a bitter, sacred incense. Her cropped hair is damp. Her legs are swollen, the large, aching ankles seem to groan as she pulls her weight along. She stands there, the great teeth throbbing in her round, gleaming face. Oh, Ida.

For a moment she is framed against her new white washing machine, as if waiting to be photographed— savage, miraculous, with the ambiguous smile of an old hearth goddess, an icon to which no offering was ever made without a grumble.

Part Ten   A GIFT for life. One I

knew who had it was murdered. That night I was living in Connecticut, in a new house containing many old objects, books and pictures rushed out of St. Petersburg in the 1920's. The letters of the Russian alphabet were everywhere, on the cover of the cookbooks over the wall oven, inside the collections of poetry next to the bed, in the tall art books stacked up near the fireplace. From new world to new world, many old things. That summer it had seemed a good idea to rent my house up in Maine, to *try* Connecticut.

On the evening news I heard his name and saw the police carrying the body, covered in a tarpaulin, out of the apartment house in the East 50's in New York. His name, full name, not quite what we called him. He, the name, the doors opening to the street, the body proceeding to the morgue, flashed by quickly in a staccato announcement like the temperature, promising to rise, the baseball scores. Switching to another channel for its sudden flash, I found him there once more. He, shot in his own apartment, in the night. A stranger? What powers strangers can make use of.

The murder was never solved and soon nothing more was heard of it. For some reason a year passed before his friends gathered themselves together and produced a delayed, mild, uncertain memorial service at St. Bartholomew's.

A murder is a challenge, an embarrassment, to the inner life of the dead one, almost a dishonor, like other violent events that may come upon you without warning. It is not certain that you may not have in some careless or driven way chosen to put yourself in the path of a murderer. Maybe for pleasure—that is the worst. The path of a murderer, there to choose. Take this street, take this hand.

His apartment was very striking. Expensive views, just what he wanted, everyone said. He had begun to make money, had only been in his splendid tower for a short time, for one large dinner party, there at last in the proper setting for his gift for life. To vanish so quickly, without knowing or telling, without the body's preparation of distress, without clues, left in this case a blank more like a natural death than death itself, with its documents of worn arteries, explosions of rampaging tumors, final minutes.

Miss Lavore. It has been many, many years since I used to see her passing in the halls of the rooming houses near Columbia. Thumping by, heavy and preoccupied, on the go, with the vanity of a truck blasting through the avenues. Miss Lavore: now, there was a warrior with red feathers in her hair and the paint of many ambushes on her full cheeks.

The houses with their separate rooms and communal kitchens and baths were lived in by female graduate students, some reading *The Faerie Queene*, and by women who went out to work each day. The working women were talkative and yet evasive in the extreme. From many rooming houses they had gathered their expertise; knowledge of sudden alliances that turned sour in a moment finally produced their chatty guardedness. In their lives, what the rooming house represented for these persons who had been in the same job for years, was the fear of the rental lease, of the acquisition of furniture.

No matter, they would put up curtains, cover the maple furniture tops with bits of cloth, add a better reading lamp to soothe the office-tired eyes.

And yet the women talked a good deal of the time about their memories of the houses of their youth. Damask Rose dishes in brackets on the wall were remembered, old lace, brass candleholders, serving spoons of coin silver, strongly ticking clocks with decorated faces, faded quilts, boxes of rosewood.

Perhaps little of it was true. Secretive persons tend to generalized memories, discreet editings, and the inevitable seasoning of sugar. Not one of the women would tell where she worked. And each one treasured the chastising sign, many times underlined: *Please Clean This Tub After Using*.

They cooked their small dinners and the wastebaskets appended the story with cracker boxes, candy wrappers, hot-dog cartons.

* * *

Miss Lavore had a life. Nearly every night of the week she went to Arthur Murray's dancing classes. A framed, autographed portrait of Murray and his wife hung over her bed. It would be florid to say it hung there like a religious icon, but certainly the two secular persons filled Miss Lavore's heart with gratitude. It could be said they had changed her life.

Miss Lavore was large and strong and homely and in her late fifties. At the end of the working day, she came home on the subway, came home alert with energy for her dancing, convivial nights. She cooked dinners rather more substantial than the usual, had a spell with the radio and the shower and then reappeared in her full-skirted dresses. They were of the brightest, harshest colors: robin's-egg blue, cherry, and kelly green. With them she wore her serviceable black suede pumps. Colored glass earrings and pins matched with her bright dresses. Coty's cologne scented her strong arms. A daunting sight.

Off she went, a member of a special ten-year Arthur Murray Club, participant in parties, anniversaries, bonus lessons, prizes and competitions. At midnight she was back once more.

The other women, seeing the shape Miss Lavore had given to her existence, timidly inquired sometimes about the possibility of sharing this night world, which could after all be purchased.

Miss Lavore had the skepticism of experience, the loftiness of her earned waltzing cups, her certificates, her souvenirs. She knew the ropes. The rustling dresses had seen service year after year.

To the ladies' questions she might reply: Have you

thought of bowling? There's a lot going there, if you have the knack of it. Under persistence, she would grant a devastating interview in the hallways, an interview in which were mixed the tolerance and hopelessness of an old clerk knowledgeable about lies.

Do you dance at all? Now tell me, what do you mean when you say you dance a little? What is a little? Tango? Rumba?

The waltz, my friend, is not as easy as it looks.

What lust there was in her eyes. "This fellow" and "that fellow" punctuated her conversation with their drumbeats. Several nights each week, she was held in the arms of many dancing partners, new members and old. At the studio there was music, fruit punch, and the touch of beards on her cheek. At the end of it all, handshakes and embraces, joshing farewells to the staff and inquisitive smiles of encouragement to the diffident beginners.

One night I was coming home on the subway and I saw her at the other end of the train. She was wrapped, it seemed, in a pleasant, hard-earned fatigue. In her hand she held a small flower-strewn box and when she opened it there was a large piece of cake, decorated with pink-and-white icing, the kind ordered for celebrations.

She ate the cake, retied the ribbon on the box and stored it away in a large black handbag, from which it would be extracted and placed on the table in her room reserved for happy memories. Happy memories, triumphs, the long ledger of her life, displayed on tables and dresser tops, tucked away in tissue paper. Adding up.

In the late evening, Miss Lavore was a transitional ghost, wandering in the indistinct moment between night and day. Over her green dress she was wearing a coat of heavy black cloth. Her green earrings dangled under a gray felt hat shaped like a pillow. A gray lock of hair touched rimless spectacles I had never seen before. She was drifting slowly into the body of the one who went out to work year after year.

Suddenly she fell asleep, lulled by the motion of the train. With a great sigh, she nodded into rest, the pillow hat slipping down her brow.

At the 110th Street station she awakened with a start, the alarm clock of experience, and gathered herself together for the push up the stairs to the street. She passed back and forth in the darkness and then in the slashes of light her earrings would shine out for a moment.

It occurred to me then that her name was probably not Lavore. That was her green and robin's-egg-blue name, not the signature of the black coat and rimless spectacles.

She is, in her dreams, part of a team and when she whirls and dips she is caught by a slim man in a black tail coat, a man with a Balkan name like people in the circus. She spins around him, brilliant as a cockatoo in a cage. They are Lavore and ——, famous European dancing team.

We passed open bars and closed shops. One corner would be deserted, as if an entire side street had turned off its lights and closed its eyes. Another would be filled with people standing in groups, alert, sleepless, looking about for the next stop of a night that had just begun. A woman in white nurse's shoes appeared in the red of the stoplight. Miss Lavore and the nurse stand side by side for a moment. They take in each other briefly. The last dying flutter of curiosity in two hearts that are already beating on the edge of sleep.

A taxi comes to the curb and a young man jumps out to buy the *Daily News* and jumps back in. Miss Lavore pauses as if struck by this cue for ways to prolong the night. But she has no interest in the news.

Whistling noises fill the air suddenly and die down once more. At last Miss Lavore and I nod in the elevator and slip into the hall of the strange apartment with its peculiar cells for the protection of a vast, overwhelming privacy. She goes to the left and I to the right. Doors open and eyes peer out to check on the intruders; the cautious hinges are squeaking out a sort of accusation.

Someone is running a bath, someone is listening to the late-night preacher on the radio. He is asking for contributions for "our ministry." Box 234 for the expenses incurred in God's work. And then a man and woman harmonize "Love Lifted Me."

. . . from the waters lifted me and safe am I . . .

It is all right. Tomorrow one of the young women will take her suitcases and leave forever, since it has never been her idea to stay beyond her purpose. For the older women it is different. They are like poor cattle herdsmen in a drought. Annoying waits in the kitchen, irritation with the habits of strangers, nightmares. What began as a green start may turn overnight into a desert filled with alarm, with impossibility. So move on. Try out a similar arrangement on Riverside Drive. But defiantly, as if to say: You cannot destroy a ruin.

1973
Dearest M.: I have sold the big house in Maine and will make a new place to live, beginning with the old

barn on the water. I will not say a new place to live newly in. Wouldn't one have to go off to something like an island for that, without newspapers, books and friends. Newness seeks a mild temperature, doesn't it? I will stay in the three or four towns of my life—and the climate rough in each in its own way.

"Existing barn," the architect's drawings say. But I fear the metamorphosis, the journey of species. The barn, or so I imagine of all barns, once existed for cows and hay. Then later it came to us, especially to him who has left, as a refuge with a menacing swallow's nest near the door.

Will the barn consent to become what I have decided to make of it? I don't know. Sometimes I am sure I am building for a tire salesman from Bangor whose wife will not be kind to the wounds of such a building—the claims, the outcry of old animals, the memories. The claims and cries of Lightolier, Design Research, colored rugs on the painted wood.

As for the other, sluffed-off house, I mourn and regret much. The nights long ago with H.W. and her worn recording of Alice Raveau in Gluck's *Orfeo*. I hear the music, see H.W. very tall, old, with her stirring maidenly beauty. The smell of the leaves outside dripping rain, the fire alive, the bowls of nasturtiums everywhere, the orange Moroccan cloth hanging over the mantle. What a loss. I will never cease to love the old lady who gave to us and to me alone so much, even to me the old house and the barn. Otherwise where would they have come from—for me? Who had no thought of Maine, so far from home.

For the rest of the loss, perhaps my memories betray me a little and bleach the darkness of the scene, the agitation of the evenings. I am as aware as anyone of the appeal, the power of the negative. Well, we go from one graven image to the next and, say what you will, each house is a shrine.

Meanwhile here in New York I just saw a horse and rider amidst the threatening taxi cabs. The man rides the horse indeed as if he were driving a cab, nervously, angrily, looking straight ahead, in his own lane. One way it is, held on the conveyor belt of traffic, needing only a horse horn of some kind to show that man may in New York turn a horse into a Dodge.

When we first came here the house opposite was a stable. A handsome brick building painted in a dusty mustard shade, like an Italian villa. Sometimes the old structure seems to return, coming out of the afternoon haze, rising from the sea of cement. But what good would the return do itself, me?

The horse and rider escaped to the park. Where old stables stood there is a parking lot. A hundred beautiful chariots rest there in the afternoon sun. And at night sometimes the car of someone I know sits there all alone, waiting for midnight.

Much love, as always,
Elizabeth

That was then, four or five years ago. The New York car has gone and in Maine the reclaimed barn now shudders in the sudden coastal winds. The white chairs on the terrace are cleaned by the mist, and the terrace itself, anxious grounding, seems slowly being washed away to the sea. The ancient white flowering bush, splendid with its murderous, curved thorns, stands guard on the bank. A handsome boat is edging toward a red plastic mooring. Goldfinches in the alders. Scenery, changing with the light in the sky. I look at it often, and often, like others here, congratulate myself for having done so.

On the battered calendar of the past, the back-glancing flow of numbers, I had imagined there would be felicitous notations of entrapments and escapes, days in the South with their insinuating feline accent, and nights in the East, showing a restlessness as beguiling as the winds of Aeolus. And myself there, marking the day with an *I*.

In truth, moments, months, even years were magical. Pages turned, answering prayers, and persons called out, Are you there? The moon changed the field to the silvery lavender of daybreak.

And yet the old pages of the days and weeks are splattered with the dark-brown rings of coffee cups and I find myself gratefully dissolved in the grounds as the water drips downward. As it must be, perhaps, for one who dislikes the theater and would instead stay at home reading the text out of which spring the actors in boots, letters on trays, and handsome women at the window, looking out on a painted backdrop of trees and factories.

At times I am not certain who is imagining the working people living in their clashing houses, lying in their landscape, as if beneath a layer of underclothes. Or those gathering rubbish, dear indeed to them as relics. Or those threading through love, missing the eye of the needle.

Words and rhythms, a waterfall of clauses, blue lights, amber eyes, the sea under a burning lake. Should I remember the perfection of a pointed chin and the abundant, prickly halo of amorous, black Levantine hair? Or my rival, the girl with the pale-green letter paper?

* * *

Oh, M., when I think of the people I have buried, North and South. Yet, why is it that we cannot keep the note of irony, the jangle of carelessness at a distance? Sentences in which I have tried for a certain light tone— many of those have to do with events, upheavals, destructions that caused me to weep like a child.

> . . . O you could not know
> That such swift fleeing
> No soul foreseeing—
> Not even I—would undo me so!

Mother, the reading glasses and the assignation near the clammy faces, so gray, of the intense church ladies. And then a lifetime with its mound of men climbing on and off.

The torment of personal relations. Nothing new there except in the disguise, and in the escape on the wings of adjectives. Sweet to be pierced by daggers at the end of paragraphs.

Sometimes I resent the glossary, the concordance of truth, many have about my real life, have like an extra pair of spectacles. I mean that such fact is to me a hindrance to memory.

Otherwise I love to be known by those I care for. *Public assistance*, beautiful phrase. Thus, I am always on the phone, always writing letters, always waking up to address myself to B. and D. and C.—those whom I dare not ring up until morning and yet must talk to throughout the night.

VIRAGO MODERN CLASSICS

The first Virago Modern Classic, *Frost in May* by Antonia White, was published in 1978. It launched a list dedicated to the celebration of women writers and to the rediscovery and reprinting of their works. Its aim was, and is, to demonstrate the existence of a female tradition in fiction which is both enriching and enjoyable. The Leavisite notion of the 'Great Tradition', and the narrow, academic definition of a 'classic', has meant the neglect of a large number of interesting secondary works of fiction. In calling the series 'Modern Classics' we do not necessarily mean 'great' — although this is often the case. Published with new critical and biographical introductions, books are chosen for many reasons: sometimes for their importance in literary history; sometimes because they illuminate particular aspects of womens' lives, both personal and public. They may be classics of comedy or storytelling; their interest can be historical, feminist, political or literary.

Initially the Virago Modern Classics concentrated on English novels and short stories published in the early decades of this century. As the series has grown it has broadened to include works of fiction from different centuries, different countries, cultures and literary traditions. In 1984 the Victorian Classics were launched; there are separate lists of Irish, Scottish, European, American, Australian and other English speaking countries; there are books written by Black women, by Catholic and Jewish women, and a few relevant novels by men. There is, too, a companion series of Non-Fiction Classics constituting biography, autobiography, travel, journalism, essays, poetry, letters and diaries.

By the end of 1986 over 250 titles will have been published in these two series, many of which have been suggested by our readers.